To Ellodie

Best wishes

Jonny Tucker

D0715989

Jonny Zucker writes for children, teenagers and adults. His first novel for Piccadilly was the teen title *One Girl, Two Decks, Three Degrees of Love*, which was serialised by BBC radio. Jonny lives in North London with his wife and young children.

The Venus Spring series:

Venus Spring – Stunt Girl
Venus Spring – Body Double
Venus Spring – Star Turn
Venus Spring – Face Off

Venus Spring

Face ★ Off

JONNY ZUCKER

PICCADILLY PRESS • LONDON

For all staff and pupils at:
Netley Primary
Lea Valley Primary
Preston Park Primary

Massive thanks to Ruth Williams, Melissa Patey,
Brenda Gardner and the rest of the Piccadilly crew for supporting
Venus on all her travels.

First published in Great Britain in 2008
by Piccadilly Press Ltd.,
5 Castle Road, London NW1 8PR
www.piccadillypress.co.uk

A catalogue record for this book is available from the British Library

ISBN: 978 1 85340 977 6 (paperback)

1 3 5 7 9 10 8 6 4 2

Printed in the UK by CPI Bookmarque, Croydon, CR0 4TD
Cover design by Simon Davis
Cover illustration by Nicola Taylor

Set in 11.5 point Palatino and Avant Garde

Chapter One

I'm watching you.

Venus Spring stared at the inside of her school locker door in horror. Taped next to her pictures of legendary kickboxing heroes and her favourite stunt artist, Kelly Tanner, was a piece of lined paper, bearing these terrifying words.

This would have been unnerving and scary enough, but the spindly handwriting sent particular tremors of fear through Venus's body. She'd recognise that writing anywhere – it belonged to her arch-enemy, Franco Dane.

Franco had been at her grandfather Dennis's stunt camp in the summer. Venus had gone to the camp to learn stunt skills and have fun, but while there she'd uncovered a plot that Franco was caught up in, along with his mother. Venus had thwarted the plot but Franco's mother had died in a plane explosion after an airborne fight with Venus – an explosion that Venus had been very, very lucky to escape.

Venus had been convinced that Franco was also dead, but on her return home from stunt camp she'd received a postcard in his distinctive, spindly writing saying *See you soon*. This had completely spooked her; she knew the tone of the postcard was deeply menacing – not only was he alive but he was on her case. In the intervening two and a half months, thoughts of him had continued to haunt her and she had often imagined she'd seen him. Once, she'd even chased someone believing it to be Franco and then suffered huge embarrassment when it turned out to be someone else.

But here was that distinctive writing again. And yet again, the message seemed both menacing and threatening to Venus. She had been to her locker only ten minutes before, but she'd forgotten a file and had quickly returned to it. This meant that the note had been been stuck up in the interim, which meant Franco must be fairly close by; perhaps he was even watching her now . . .

Venus shivered uncontrollably. She looked both ways down the corridor. To her left a group of younger boys were swapping football trading cards outside the first floor gym; to her right a sixth form girl was speaking on her mobile and twisting her hair in her fingers.

Venus looked at the note again and a knot of anxiety twisted in stomach.

'Hey you lot,' she called over to the boys. 'Did any of you see a tall guy with dark hair hanging round my locker?'

The boys shook their heads and returned to their cards.

Venus tried to reassure herself, but she couldn't.

Can I really be one hundred per cent sure the note is from Franco? No. Do I think very, very strongly it's from him? Yes. If it is from him, how the hell did he get inside my locker? And for that matter, how did he know which is my locker? If he can get inside my locker, he can get anywhere.

Her hand trembling, Venus pulled off the note and quickly put it into her jacket pocket. She could hardly bear to touch something that Franco had touched. She was desperate to talk to someone who would understand her terror – and that was her best friend and next-door neighbour, Kate Fox.

Kate was in the year above Venus. She was an ideal best mate – they shared lots of interests, particularly music and sport, and she was an excellent listener who knew almost every secret Venus had ever had.

Venus found Kate in the ground floor gym. Kate was doing a warm up with some other people. They were about to go on a run for their afternoon's PE lesson.

As Venus strode across the polished wood floor, Kate looked up and spotted her. She immediately hurried over to Venus.

'Hey, Venus,' Kate said, smiling. 'You look as if the world's about to end. What's up?'

'I just found this in my locker,' replied Venus, trying to sound casual. She held out the piece of lined paper for Kate to see. Kate's smile was immediately wiped off her face.

'Oh my God, that's horrible.'

'I think it's from Franco.'

Kate took the piece of paper in her hands. 'Seriously?'

'Remember that postcard I got from him just before we went to France?'

'Of course. This handwriting is similar.'

'It's *too* similar to be a coincidence, don't you think? The guy's stalking me.'

Kate took a deep breath and sat down on a low wooden bench, patting the space beside her for her friend to sit. Venus was almost in tears as she described finding the note, but just talking to Kate made her feel a bit better.

'Look, Venus,' Kate said, handing the note back. 'I know you had a terrible experience with him in the summer. But this note might be completely unconnected. You know there are quite a few freaks in this place. It could be from someone who fancies you or it could be a joke.'

Venus shook her head. 'If you fancy someone you don't go scaring the life out of them and if it is a joke it's a pretty bad one.'

Kate had listened intently to Venus and she thought for a few moments before speaking again. 'Don't bite my head off,' she said slowly, 'but remember that you have imagined seeing Franco a few times recently.'

Venus felt herself shaking. 'Exactly! Maybe he has been following me, and look at the writing! It's got to be him.'

'Hey,' said Kate, putting her arm round her friend's shoulder. 'All I'm saying is, don't jump to conclusions and switch to emergency mode instantly. It could be from him, but it's more likely not to be. You are very, very sensitive to any Franco news.'

Venus scratched her forehead. *Kate's right. I am extra*

sensitive to any hint of Franco and maybe I'm being paranoid. But if it isn't from him, then who wrote it?

'Hey, Venus,' Kate said as the bell for afternoon lessons went. 'Let's talk after school, yeah?'

'Hi, Venus, I'm home!'

Venus was up in her bedroom listening to music when she heard the front door opening. She'd spent the whole of the afternoon trying to focus on her lessons and not think about the note – with limited success. Straight after school she'd gone round to Kate's and they'd talked more about the note and the chances of it being from someone else other than Franco. After a while, they'd started going round and round in circles, so they'd dropped the subject and discussed the next gig they wanted to go to. Venus had then come back home and spent an hour chilling out, listening to music, desperately trying to put all thoughts of Franco out of her mind.

Venus sighed deeply. Things between her and her mum, Gail, had been seriously strained over the last few weeks. And all of this tension centred on Venus's American father, Elliot Nevis.

Elliot had walked out on Venus and Gail when Venus was three months old. Venus knew this because her mum had told her. She'd also told Venus that Elliot had gone back to America and never contacted her again.

But Venus had recently found out that this wasn't totally true.

Just over a month ago, Venus had actually met Elliot, thanks to Dennis – Gail's father. Elliot had come to England on business and he'd asked Dennis if he could set up a meeting between father and daughter.

So they'd met.

And after her initial bursts of fury at Elliot for leaving her and her mum, she'd started to listen to him and realised that he'd had no choice but to leave, and that Gail had told him to stay out of their lives.

Venus had felt terribly guilty being in contact with her dad behind her mum's back, but she couldn't see any way round it. She knew that Gail hated Elliot. Things had come to a head just before Elliot was due to return to the States. Venus had gone to meet him in a café and Gail, feeling that Venus was up to something, had followed her and found them both.

Venus had made herself scarce while her parents talked to each other for the first time in fourteen years. Venus later found out from each of them separately, that 'talked' was a very pleasant way of describing their dialogue. Gail had immediately started attacking

Elliot about his outrageous behaviour in contacting Venus. Elliot had insisted he had every right to see his daughter; he was her father and at fourteen years of age, Venus was capable of deciding whether or not she wanted to be in touch with him.

This 'meeting' had lasted fifteen minutes and ended acrimoniously. Within a few hours, Elliot was on a plane returning to the States and Gail was left fuming. The following days had been especially awful and Venus and Gail spent hours arguing about everything. The atmosphere at home had been fraught with tension and bitterness ever since.

While Gail was devastated that Venus had been seeing Elliot behind her back and that her own father, Dennis, had stayed in touch with Elliot for all these years and organised their meeting, Venus was devastated that Gail had lied to her about the real reason for Elliot's departure. He'd told her that he'd desperately tried to make things work with Gail. Venus had always trusted Gail but now that trust had been shattered. It felt like Gail had stolen a huge chunk of her life.

Since meeting him, Venus had decided that she was more like Elliot than Gail. Elliot was some kind of 'fixer' who investigate problems and sorted them out. Gail was a high-flying lawyer who desperately wanted

Venus to follow in her legal footsteps. But Venus was intent on becoming a stunt artist like her granddad, Dennis – and Elliot could understand that. Venus spent as much time as possible learning how to do stunts from her granddad, hanging out on film sets with him and keeping fit for her stunt skills. She had kept her stunt life secret from Gail because she knew her mum would disapprove of such potentially dangerous work, and would do her best to stop her. If she'd known what Venus had already got up to with her stunt life, she would have grounded her until her eighteenth birthday. As a result, Gail knew nothing about Franco.

Dennis had left for Peru a week ago; he was working as the stunt co-ordinator on a high budget American film about a group of mercenaries attempting to overthrow a despotic ruler. He'd texted Venus a couple of times since he'd got there, but he was obviously very busy and she missed his reassuring presence deeply.

So Venus and Gail were alone in London together, living in the same house and trying to lead a normal day-to-day existence. Elliot's name hadn't been mentioned for two days and that was something of a record. But the tension was still simmering away and the cauldron of anger and recriminations could boil over at any minute.

'I've done us Mexican,' said Gail overly brightly when Venus strolled into the kitchen. Gail was giving her a lot of these forced smiles at the moment; she was determined to make things OK between the two of them. 'And I've been looking at some of these catalogues . . .'

Venus nodded but she was in her own world – where threatening notes inside lockers took precedence over all else, no matter how hard she tried to push them to the back of her mind.

'. . . What do you think, Venus?'

Venus looked up at Gail. 'Sorry?'

'. . . About going late night shopping? I was just saying about these catalogues – there are some good sales on. I could meet you one night after work. What do you reckon?'

'Yeah, sure, sounds good,' Venus said, nodding. She sat down at the kitchen table and took a bite from a nacho. She looked at her mum who was crouching by the oven and checking the chilli con carne inside. Venus did her best to make polite conversation over supper. She appreciated her mum making an effort, and felt bad about not being more responsive, but thoughts of Franco kept invading her brain. In spite of Kate's warning about jumping too hastily to conclusions, Venus was sure the note was from him and that meant not only had he been in her school and found her locker but, as his note said, he was watching her. As she looked out of the kitchen window, she couldn't help wondering if that included right now.

Chapter Two

For the next few days, whenever possible, Venus was never very far from her locker. She checked it frequently each day but a second note didn't appear. A few times she thought she actually caught sight of Franco in the distance – but eventually realised this was almost certainly her imagination. She started to relax a tiny bit. When a week had passed without incident, she was able to consider the fact that she might have been wrong. Maybe the note was from someone else. Maybe it wasn't even intended for her – perhaps it was someone who'd got the wrong locker. Falling back into her daily routine, Venus was able to push the whole episode to the back of her mind.

But then something happened that really frightened her . . .

It had been a decent day in school. She'd got a B+ for

the history assignment she'd completed for the harsh Mr Carlton. She downloaded some brilliant new soul tracks from iTunes after school and there'd been an e-mail from Jed, the cute boy she'd met at her granddad's stunt camp, waiting for her when she got in.

Gail ate supper that night in record time. She was working on a big case involving a man who'd been imprisoned ten years ago for a massive bank robbery. Some new evidence had recently come to light and there was a strong suspicion that his conviction might be unsafe. Gail was his barrister and would be representing him when his appeal came to court. She was pretty certain that she'd win the case and get him released, but the paperwork for the case was colossal. She apologised to Venus for not having time to chat and retreated upstairs to her office.

Venus had seen her mum in action a couple of times. Gail looked impressive in her smart black robes and wig, and she spoke very confidently and eloquently in court, but Venus knew her own career plans involved jumping off high towers and leaping through burning buildings, not labouring over reams of paper and performing in front of a jury.

Venus went up to bed at ten-fifteen p.m. in an excellent mood. She read a couple of articles from a running magazine, sent Dennis a text and listened to the new songs on her iPod. By eleven p.m. she was fast asleep.

She was woken by a muffled thudding sound.

Was that noise in my dream or was it in the house?

She rubbed her eyes and pulled herself upright.

Then she heard another almost identical sound.

No, it wasn't in my dream. Is Mum still up?

Venus looked at her alarm clock. *03.17* the red digital numbers declared. Gail could possibly still be up, but even for her this would be very, very late. Venus strained to hear if there were any more sounds, but couldn't detect any. Slipping out of bed she quickly crossed her room. She grabbed the nearest potential weapon she could see – her tennis racket, which was wedged into the narrow gap beside her wardrobe – just in case.

She turned her bedroom door handle very slowly and tiptoed out onto the landing. Gail's bedroom door was closed – which suggested she'd gone to bed – but a strip of light was coming from the gap below her office door. Perhaps her mum was still working after all. Taking a deep breath, Venus crept over to the office door, and put her ear against it. No sound came from within.

OK. I don't want to give any warning if someone's in there.

Venus tightened her grip on the tennis racket and curled the fingers of her free hand round the door knob. Her breathing sped up and in one swift movement she forcefully turned the door knob and burst into the room.

It was empty.

But she immediately noticed that the net curtains were blowing inwards. Venus closed the door to make sure no one would creep in behind her, then hurried across the room and pushed the curtains aside. The window was half open – wide enough for someone to climb through, if they could negotiate the drainpipe. She looked outside. There was no sign of anyone in the yard below or out in the street, but Venus had the horrible feeling that someone had been in this room, and an image of Franco swept into her mind.

It was then that she noticed the glimmer of Gail's desk light. Venus stepped over to it. On the desk were some chunky grey files, her work diary and two pieces of paper, neatly laid out side by side, which was the way Gail liked things to be – ordered and accessible.

Venus looked at the papers. One listed firms of solicitors her mother was currently working with: *Dalefords, Cobhams, Wheel & Trotter, Stevenson May, Fordwich & Lime*; the second was an expenses sheet: *Admin – £678; Taxis – £356; Rail – £234.59; Maintenance – £1,062.* The diary listed her appointments with clients along with the times and locations; her mum was certainly busy over the next few weeks, Venus registered – she was going all over the place, to Battle Lane Law Centre, Tufnell Avenue, Fenford Prison, Golam Tower, Rining Young Offenders Centre . . .

Suddenly her heart jumped as she heard the tiny squeak of the door knob. Closing the diary, she looked across the room and saw it slowly turning. Every muscle in Venus's body tightened. She gripped the tennis racket harder and moved swiftly and silently back across the room.

The door began to creak open. Venus raised the racket in the air, ready to attack. As she did so she realised it was far too light to be much of a weapon. Suddenly the door swung open the rest of the way as a figure lurched into the room and Venus came face-to-face with . . . Gail.

'Oh my God!' Venus gasped. 'You gave me such a shock!'

'I gave you a shock?' cried Gail. 'What about me? What are you doing in here? It's nearly half past three. I thought we had an intruder.'

'That's what I thought too,' replied Venus, lowering the racket. 'I heard some odd noises so I came to investigate.'

Gail looked over Venus's shoulder with a frown. 'Why's the window open?' she observed quickly.

Venus felt an icy shiver of fear snake down her spine. 'Didn't you open it?' she demanded. And did you leave the desk light on, Mum? It was on when I came in.'

'Hey, Venus,' said Gail with a concerned expression, noting the terror in Venus's voice. 'Don't panic. I remember now – I did open the window a bit, earlier, as I was getting drowsy, and I guess I must have left it open, and the light on, too. You know I've got loads on my mind at the moment.'

'What if you didn't? What if someone broke in?'

Gail frowned and quickly inspected the room. 'Everything's *exactly* as I left it,' she said, reassuringly.

'Maybe they were after something downstairs,' pointed out Venus, anxiously.

'Have you been watching too many cop shows?' asked Gail, smiling.

'No,' replied Venus testily. 'Let's check the rest of the house.'

Together, mother and daughter systematically went round the house, looking inside each room. But the whole place was completely untouched.

'It's fine,' said Gail as they walked back upstairs together. 'There's no intruder. Everything's in place and there's absolutely no sign of a break in. I just left the window of my office open and left the light on; it's no big deal, OK?'

Venus wasn't convinced. Whatever she might say, her mum just wasn't the forgetful type. 'What about the thuds I heard?' she asked.

Gail smiled and put her arm round Venus's shoulder. 'It must have been from outside; we all hear sounds from the street and think they're inside the house, but they're not. Now let's go back to bed and get some sleep. If we stay up any longer we'll both be complete wrecks in the morning.'

Venus sighed and headed back to her room. However much her mum had tried to reassure her, she felt deeply uneasy about the whole episode.

I'm watching you.

Venus couldn't help but remember the words on the note. She was deeply agitated by the night's events and it wasn't until four-thirty a.m. that she finally fell into a fitful and disturbed slumber.

Thank goodness it was the weekend.

'I've got a really bad feeling about this.'

Kate Fox looked at Venus with concern. Venus had gone round to Kate's first thing on Saturday morning to tell her about the incident in the early hours.

'But your mum said she probably left the window open and wouldn't be too surprised if she'd left the light on?' Kate said encouragingly.

'Yeah.'

'And nothing was touched in the whole house?'

'No, but —'

'And you said you didn't see anyone outside.'

Venus sighed deeply. Listening to Kate in the cold light of day did make it sound like a total non-event.

'Look, Venus, even if Franco wasn't in the house, it is a horrible thought and this, plus the note, is freaking you out. I think you should give that police woman friend of yours a call – you know, DCI Radcliff – see what she thinks about it all.'

A few months ago, Venus hadn't even heard of Carla Radcliff, but now she was a key player in Venus's life. It was Radcliff who'd dealt with the plot at Dennis's stunt camp, Radcliff who'd sent Venus on the Body Double case; and Radcliff who'd picked up the pieces after Venus and her father had stopped a catastrophe just before the premiere of *Airborne Sword*.

'Maybe I will,' said Venus.

When she got back home Venus left a message on Radcliff's mobile. She tried to keep her voice calm but talking about what happened made her relive her panic and fear, so she rushed her words and let Radcliff know in no uncertain terms, that she thought Franco was after her. Ten minutes later she got a text asking her to meet the DCI outside the British

Museum in an hour. Venus told her mum she was popping into town to get some new trainers.

'Great,' replied Gail, 'I'll come with you; I need a couple of things. We could hang out together.'

'Er . . . no, Mum, you won't want to hang out with me. I'll need to go to loads of sports shops and try on hundreds of pairs; it will be ultra boring.'

'OK,' Gail said, laughing. 'I get the message: *Teenage girl embarrassed to be seen in public with her mother.*'

'It's not like that, Mum,' protested Venus.

'It doesn't matter. I can't face it really; all of those crowds on a Saturday. Are you sure *you* want to go?'

Venus felt bad. Her mother was trying to improve their relationship and she didn't want to snub her. But Gail knew nothing about her activities with Carla Radcliff and she wanted to keep it that way. Her mum was under enough stress.

The tube was very busy and, emerging out into the street from Tottenham Court Road station, Venus was near mobbed by great throngs of people. Tourists mingled with people looking for early Christmas presents, foreign students handed out leaflets and dejected-looking individuals held huge boards advertising low price carpets and cheap Chinese food buffets.

Venus headed off down Tottenham Court Road, took a right turn and two minutes later found herself standing outside the impressive entrance to the British Museum. DCI Radcliff was sitting on the steps reading a newspaper. She was wearing a black trouser suit and crisp white shirt and her hair was scraped back tightly off her face. She stood up when she spotted Venus.

'Let's go inside,' said Radcliff.

They went in, had their respective bags checked by security and were waved through.

'You sounded very perturbed in your message,' said Radcliff as they walked past some Ancient Egyptian artefacts. 'You said Franco was stalking you?'

'I found this on the inside of my locker at school,' said Venus, handing over the note.

Radcliff took it and studied it for a few seconds without breaking her stride.

'Are you sure it's from him?'

'It's his handwriting,' replied Venus.

'Could be from someone with very similar handwriting,' pointed out Radcliff.

Venus shook her head. 'I've checked it with the writing on the postcard I got from him in the summer; they're near enough identical.'

'So you found this note in your locker and you think

it's from Franco. That's a pretty disturbing concept. What else has happened?'

They stopped in front of a large display of papyrus.

'I've caught glimpses of him over the past months, and last night I heard a couple of thuds coming from my mum's office. The light was on and the window was open. Mum said she probably left them like that, but I'm not so sure.'

'Was anything taken?' asked Radcliff.

'No.'

'Was anything moved?'

'No.'

'Was anything damaged?'

'No, but I've got this horrible feeling that he'd been in the house.' Even as she was saying this, Venus realised how feeble her claims must sound to the DCI.

Radcliff pursed her lips. 'So this is where we're up to: a note taped to your locker that you think is from Franco, a few possible sightings of him, and a "feeling" that Franco was in your house last night although nothing whatsoever was taken or disturbed.'

Venus frowned. She could sense that Radcliff was trying to control her impatience. 'I think he's stalking me; I think I might need protection.'

Radcliff turned to face her. 'Venus, you're a very talented and sensible girl, and I've been very impressed by your bravery and resourcefulness, but I have to look at this from a police point of view. The note *could* have been from Franco and he *might* have been in your house last night. But you've had a really hard time recently and it would be easy for your imagination to run away with you.'

'The note's not my imagination,' replied Venus, trying to keep the anger out of her voice.

'I know that,' responded Radcliff impassively. 'But even if it was Franco who left the note, it's unpleasant, but not illegal. At this stage, we have no *proof* that Franco's committing any crime. I sympathise with you completely but until I have evidence that he's actively involved in some wrongdoing, I won't be able to dedicate any police resources to the matter. I can't offer you protection when I'm not sure there's anything to protect you against.'

Venus felt her whole body deflate.

'Look Venus, I'll always take your calls. And obviously at the first scrap of evidence that Franco Dane is stalking you, I will act with speed – I promise you. But at this stage, I'm afraid there's nothing to go on so I can't do anything.'

Venus clenched her fists in frustration. 'How can I get any proof if he doesn't hang around long enough to be seen?' she demanded.

'That situation faces me every day of my working life, Venus. Criminals tend to try to *not* get caught, so it's endlessly frustrating and time-consuming to nail them. Even at Dennis's stunt camp, we found no definite proof linking Franco to the countryside poison plot, however certain we all are that he was involved.'

Venus sighed heavily.

Radcliff thinks I'm just some over-anxious school-kid.

They walked in silence back through the gallery, across the giant entrance hall and out into the courtyard.

'Call me whenever you like,' said Radcliff, giving Venus a nod, 'and I'll take anything you say seriously, but like I said – I need *proof*.'

And with that, Radcliff turned and swept away over the courtyard and out into the street where a sleek black car was waiting for her. She climbed inside and closed the door. A few seconds later, the car pulled away. Venus stood where she was and watched until it had disappeared from view.

Venus left the courtyard and a couple of minutes later found herself back on Tottenham Court Road. She walked down the street looking, unseeingly, at the window displays of the long line of electronics shops. She felt distraught that Radcliff hadn't been able to help her. What was she going to do now? She thought back a few months to her face off with Franco in the barn – the cold look in his eyes as he moved in to attack her. She was sure he wouldn't hesitate to hurt her – or worse. Venus walked aimlessly, feeling more and more helpless and dejected. With Kate and Radcliff telling her it was probably nothing, Dennis in Peru and Elliot in America, she felt that she had no one to turn to for help now. As the crowds of shoppers swirled about her, Venus had never felt so alone.

Chapter Three

One morning the following week, at the end of break, Venus was climbing the stairs in the maths block when she happened to glance through a narrow side window. The sight that met her eyes froze her in her tracks.

There, a few metres away by the side gates of the school and partially hidden by the overhanging branches of a tree was a tall figure. He had his back to her, but she could see he had the same build and hair as Franco. And the trainers he was wearing were identical to the pair Franco had worn during a night activity at stunt camp.

Her heart lurched wildly.

Is it him? Surely it's got to be.

As she stood, frozen to the spot, the figure began to jog away from the school in the direction of Plant

Street. Venus made a snap decision. How dare he make her feel worried and vulnerable all the time – she couldn't live like that. Here was a chance to turn the tables on him – if Radcliff wanted proof of Franco's wrongdoings, she'd get it. Venus sped back down the stairs and burst through the outside double doors. By now, he'd be nearing Plant Street and she probably wouldn't catch him if she took the same route.

Sprinting forward, Venus dashed along the concrete walkway that snaked down the side of the school, ducking down as she passed the site manager's office without breaking her stride. Luckily for her, no one was about. After about fifty metres she reached the corner and sprung forward, grasping the railings with both hands and quickly propelling herself upwards. She swung over the top and jumped down, landing with a thud on the pavement below.

She was so determined not to lose the trail that she ran straight out into the road, only seeing a low silver sports car speeding right towards her at the last second. The driver beeped his horn frantically. In one swift movement, Venus flung herself into the air and slid across the car's bonnet. She rolled off onto the pavement to break her fall. It was a well-known stunt move that she'd practised with Dennis, but the driver didn't seem to appreciate her talents and screamed obscenities at her. But Venus didn't look back. She was aleady up on her feet again and running hard down an alley, the wooden fences on either side flashing past. She emerged on Plant Street.

There was no sign of Franco.

A feeling of desperation washed over her, but she sprinted to the end of Plant Street to the T-junction that met the High Street. Looking left, she only saw shoppers and someone selling cheap watches. Looking right, she saw more shoppers. She cursed, reluctantly accepting defeat.

Oh well, maybe it wasn't Franco after all, she thought, trying to appease herself.

And then she saw him. He was hurrying past the betting shop. Venus felt a surge of adrenaline. She pulled her beanie hat out of her jacket and put it on firmly, squashing all of her hair well inside. Then she pulled up the hood of her jacket and wrapped up her scarf around her mouth. It wasn't much of a disguise but hopefully it would protect her if he looked round. She could still only see his back, but his long easy strides were all too familiar.

Terror and excitement fought within her, uncertainty gnawed at her, but nothing was going to stop her now.

He passed the fruit stall, the bookshop and the fried

chicken shack and then turned off the High Street into a small dead-end road. Venus hurried after him. He was no more than thirty metres in front. He headed for the opening of a small alley at the end. Venus followed.

When she reached the end of the alley, she couldn't see him at first. But then she spotted him traversing a road that cut across a small, dilapidated square. He then crossed over a railway bridge. Venus had never been this way before and she forced herself to suppress a growing feeling of anxiety at being in an unknown area on the trail of a boy who detested her and was probably planning to exact his revenge on her at this very second.

She passed over the bridge as a tube train sped by beneath her. He walked towards a deserted five-a-side football pitch and crossed over the peeling Astroturf. This was a big, wide open space and Venus didn't want to make herself vulnerable so she hung back. As she watched him he disappeared into another narrow alleyway. She ran after him, skirting the edge of the pitch, and then stopped at the mouth of the alleyway.

She could hear voices coming from about twenty metres ahead. As she edged forwards, her body pressed against the right hand wall of the alleyway behind some crates, the voices became clearer.

'So what's the deal with tomorrow night's job?' asked a female voice. 'I thought we were all ready to go?'

'That's what I thought,' replied a male voice. His voice was definitely not Franco's and Venus wasn't sure if she felt disappointed or not. 'I don't know why we needed to meet now.'

'I'll tell you why,' answered another male voice.

Venus felt icy prickles of apprehension all over her body. She was shaking and thought for a second that her legs would just crumble beneath her. But she steadied herself and controlled her breathing.

That voice.

It was *his* voice.

It was Franco.

'Something's come up,' said Franco, 'so I won't be there with you.'

'Hang on a second,' said the female voice. 'You said it was a three person job.'

'I know,' said Franco smoothly, 'but the two of you will just have to manage without me.'

Venus concentrated on every word until her phone suddenly bleeped a text alert and her stomach hit the ground.

Why didn't I switch it off?

'What was that?' demanded the female.

Venus heard the noise of feet tramping over stones.

In a flash, she scampered back down the alley, turned left and threw herself into a clump of bushes. Her heart was thudding like a hammer. She waited a minute, but no one appeared.

She took a deep breath and emerged from the bushes and poked her head back round into the alley.

The voices reached her ears again.

They're still there.

'So what are we going to do?' the female asked.

'We still go ahead,' replied the other male.

'What, with a person down?' she asked.

'He said he's working on it,' pointed out the male, 'and if that doesn't work out, I've got a few leads. We'll find someone.'

Venus waited for Franco to speak, but he didn't.

'Let's get out of here,' said the female voice.

'Fine by me,' agreed the male.

Venus bit her lip as she heard the sound of footsteps retreating. Very slowly she stole forwards and stuck her head round the corner, where the voices had been coming from.

I don't believe it!

A boy and a girl, a couple of years older than her she reckoned, were strolling away, but Franco wasn't with them.

Venus cursed herself.

He must have gone when I ran back down the alleyway and hid in the bushes.

Venus tried to overcome her disappointment and focused on the task in hand.

The boy was tall with close-cropped hair. He was wearing jeans, a black jacket and black trainers, and she could just make out a small tattoo of a bird on the back of his neck. The girl was average height. She had long auburn hair and she was wearing a baseball cap, jeans, a long-sleeved white T-shirt and white trainers.

They were walking quickly.

Venus silently trailed them through a couple of side streets. They then took a left and crossed a main road, before turning into a dead-end road called April Street. The houses on April Street were three-storey Victorian terraces with elaborate stonework. They all looked identical – like they'd been constructed on the same day out of a kit.

Venus hid behind a huge oak tree and watched as the boy and girl stopped outside number 32 – the third from last house on the left. The front of the house at the end – number 36 – was covered in scaffolding.

Venus saw the boy pull a key out of his pocket, turn it in the lock and open the door. They both went in and the door slammed shut behind them. Venus hurried towards the front door. Number 32 had three buzzers next to the front door. The bottom one said *Wiltons*, the middle one said *Steve Highfield*, the third had no name.

Venus stepped back and spotted a light coming on in the top floor flat. So now she knew where these two had gone. What should she do now? She glanced at her watch and realised she'd left the school premises an hour and a half ago! She'd missed lunch hour and by now afternoon lessons would have started! She had to get back immediately and come up with a plausible excuse. It was then that she realised she had no idea where April Street was in relation to school or anywhere else for that matter.

Venus texted Kate. Thank goodness Kate had a free lesson, so within moments Venus's phone beeped, alerting her to an incoming message. Kate had checked out the location on one of the IT centre's computers and she'd sent Venus directions back to school. Venus ran all the way and just made it in time for her English class.

Luckily no one mentioned Venus's earlier absence. For the rest of the afternoon she kept her head down, mulling over a plan. She would go back to April Street that night and see if she could somehow get inside the top floor flat without being seen. Perhaps she could get some information on Franco – at least his address, say. OK, so her methods wouldn't be completely complying with the laws of the country, but desperate times demanded desperate measures. And she was desperate; desperate to sort out the Franco problem once and for all.

Venus didn't speak a word of her plan to Kate; Kate was bound to attempt to talk her out of it. It was dangerous and reckless and foolish. But Venus knew it was what she needed to do – and nothing was going to dissuade her.

She was extra attentive to her mum at supper. She asked her some thoughtful questions about her current case and in turn made sure she provided Gail with plenty of detail about her day in school; parents loved that stuff.

'I'm going out with a couple of girls from school tonight,' she casually informed Gail as she cleared the supper things off the table.

Gail frowned. 'You know I'm not keen on you going out midweek,' she replied as they loaded the dishwasher. 'You're still only fourteen.'

'Come on, Mum, I hardly ever go out in the week. It's just there's this film we really want to see and it's cheap tickets tonight.'

'Who are *we*?'

Venus had her cover story perfectly formed. 'It's Tanya and Yasmin,' she explained, deliberately picking two of the 'sensible' girls who met with Gail's approval; it would be a mistake to say Kate as Gail might easily mention the film to her at some point.

Gail sighed. 'What time does it finish?'

'Five past ten. I'll be back by ten-thirty at the latest.'

Gail considered this thoughtfully. 'OK.' She nodded reluctantly. 'But it's straight to bed when you get home.'

'Yes, Mother,' Venus said, smiling.

At seven-thirty, Venus left the house, took her bike and cycled up the road. She hardly ever cycled at night, but having her own transport would give her far greater flexibility. An icy wind bit into her cheeks. Cycling at full speed it took her fifteen minutes to reach April Street. Venus locked her bike against some railings at the top of the road. She strolled down the street, casually looking over her shoulder a couple of times to see if anyone was following her.

Venus noticed there were lights on in the ground floor flat at number 32 and darkness on the first and second floors, but she walked on to number 36 – the house with the scaffolding rig.

Venus stared up at the mesh of steel bars, nuts and bolts that stretched upwards on the front of 36. She chewed her bottom lip for a few seconds, calculating the route. Then she closed her eyes for a few seconds and collected her thoughts.

Venus reached for the metal bar and pulled herself up onto the first set of wooden boarding. She'd had lots of experience scaling walls and this would be easy by comparison – at least the climbing bit would. When she'd been with Dennis on the set of *The Scales of the Pharaoh*, he'd let her climb the gigantic mocked up façade of the front of Cleopatra's palace. Even though she'd worn a safety harness it felt very dangerous. But Venus had found the whole experience exhilarating and she'd felt amazing when she reached the top and looked down at the small figures scurrying across the studio floor below.

Making as little noise as possible, Venus grabbed the next section of steel and pulled herself further upwards. The ground and first floor flats of number 36 were totally shrouded in darkness, so they were almost certainly empty. It was the second floor flat that she was worried about. The lights shining out meant that in all likelihood there were people inside and being caught shinning up someone's scaffolding at night would almost certainly result in a swift phone call to the police. However, she was wearing dark clothing – even if there was someone in the room they wouldn't spot her unless they came very close to the window.

She reached the beam below the top section of metal – just underneath the windows of the second floor flat.

Easing herself up a fraction she stole a look through the bottom of the window. A bearded man of about sixty was standing at a sink washing dishes. On the far side of the room a rosy-cheeked woman of similar years was sitting at a table writing a letter. Venus lowered her head again and waited a couple of minutes.

When she raised her head again, the man was putting a saucepan onto a drying rack. As soon as he'd done this he went over to the sofa at the far right of the room, sat down, and picked up the TV remote. As the screen flickered to life, the man seemed instantly engrossed in whatever programme he was watching. The woman looked like she was fiercely concentrating on her writing.

Venus took a deep breath and, reaching up to the next length of steel, pulled her body towards it, all the while keeping a careful eye on the flat's inhabitants. She found the beam with her feet and stepped up a level. She was now completely exposed and was about to move on when the woman suddenly stood up, put her pen down and walked straight over to the kitchenette.

Venus quickly reached to the beam beside her but there was a sharp bolt where she placed her hand and she withdrew it quickly, wincing in pain. The woman was now standing directly in front of the window, and was rooting round in a high cupboard. Venus froze completely; she was no more than a metre away from the woman's face and if she looked at the window she was bound to see her.

Please don't look! Please don't look!

The woman pulled out a packet of peanuts and then turned her face fully to the window. Venus felt her heart pounding away as the woman stared out.

Oh my God! She's seen me! I need to get out of here!

But remarkably the woman stood at the window for another couple of seconds and then turned back and headed for the table. She hadn't seen her! Breathing an immense sigh of relief, Venus shuffled along to the edge of the scaffolding. Then her heart sank. The distance between 36 and the roof terrace of 34 was too far to jump. A small skylight window on the flat roof at the top of number 32 glimmered and seemed to mock her in the moonlight. She had to get to 34 to make it to 32, but the scaffolding didn't stretch far enough.

Then Venus noticed the gargoyle jutting out of the roof above number 34. It looked fairly sturdy . . . There was only one thing for it, and she didn't let herself think what would happen if she didn't manage it. She slid down a steel pole to the level below, reached for the metal bar above her head and walked her legs off the wooden plank on which she was standing. Her legs were now dangling over thin air. Tightening her grip on the metal, she began to swing her legs backwards and forwards, building momentum.

She swung back a final time and let go of the bar above her head. Her body arced quickly through the night air. She flew forwards, her hands outstretched, and swiftly closed them around the gargoyle's stone head. Not taking a chance with its age, Venus quickly reached out to number 34's roof edge, muscles screaming, and pulled herself onto the flat roof. She rested for a moment then jumped over to the flat roof of 32 and crept across to the skylight. The window was open a fraction but by curling her fingers round the edge, Venus was able to open it fully. Quickly, she climbed in and let herself fall to the floor inside.

Venus waited for a moment in the darkness, but could hear nothing. Flicking on the torch she'd brought, she saw she was in a living room. There were two beanbags by the window facing a wide screen plasma TV. A shelving unit with four sections stood next to the TV and a small round table was on the left near the door.

Venus began her search immediately. On the table were some scattered papers, but on closer inspection they were just pizza delivery leaflets, an Indian restaurant home-delivery menu and some cards advertising local taxi firms. She strode over to the shelving unit. Several CDs and DVDs were scattered over the top two sections – indie bands and action films. There was also an iPhone, an mp3 player, two chunky silver watches and a Nintendo Wii with loads of games.

Whoever lives here has got plenty of money to burn.

Venus went to the door and pushed it open slowly. She listened; still nothing. The door opened on to a narrow corridor. Venus walked through a doorway leading straight into a kitchen. There was a worktop, an oven and a small fridge in the corner. A breakfast bar jutted out from the worktop. Venus moved to the bar and looked on its surface. Next to some milk stains left by cereal bowls was a laptop, a key ring and a pair of large black gloves. She would come back to check out the laptop when she'd been round the rest of the flat; there could be useful information on it.

The corridor split into a bathroom on the left, a bedroom on the right and the flat's front door at the end. Venus stuck her head in the bathroom and pulled the light cord. There was nothing remarkable in there: a bath, a toilet, a sink and a cabinet. She opened the cabinet door and found some mouthwash and a pack of new toothbrushes.

Her hand had just pushed the bedroom door when she heard a key turn in a lock, and the flick of a switch. Suddenly the whole corridor was flooded with light. Venus looked up like a rabbit picked out by the headlamps of an advancing car.

Standing in the door were the boy and girl she'd seen earlier.

'What the . . . ?' shouted the boy.

Venus turned and raced down the corridor, into the living room, and reached for the skylight window, footsteps crashing behind her. But as she grabbed the window with her hands, a strong grip yanked at her leg and she smashed down onto the beanbags. She spun her head round. The boy was holding onto her and the girl was standing in the doorway looking shocked and furious.

Venus lashed out and kicked the boy off. He yelped in pain as her trainer connected with his face. Looking at the the skylight, Venus knew she could never make it out without one of them grabbing her.

Venus stood panting, her body in the kickboxing attack position. The boy stood opposite her, his fists out in front of him while the girl stood behind him, her face twisted with rage.

'Who the hell are you?' hissed the boy. 'And what are you doing in our flat?'

Venus's mind was racing. What on earth could she do? There were two of them, but there was still a chance of fighting her way out . . .

'Get out of my way!' snapped Venus loudly.

'How did you get in?' demanded the girl.

'I said, get out of my way!' hissed Venus, 'I haven't taken anything.'

'Check out the flat!' commanded the boy.

The girl had a quick inspection of the living room and then left to look at the other rooms. Venus and the boy stood facing each other like two prize fighters.

A few minutes later, the girl reappeared.

'Nothing's been touched,' she said.

No one said a word. The air crackled with tension.

'What were you looking for?' snarled the boy, after what seemed liked ages.

'In here?' said Venus. 'Nothing. I don't need anything from here.'

The boy and the girl exchanged a glance.

'So why are you here?' demanded the girl.

Venus knew she had to come up with some sort of reason to avoid their further suspicion – however implausible. She'd thought of a few possible cover stories and one came to mind.

'This place is just my way in,' Venus said, trying to sound surly. 'It's the Wiltons in the ground floor flat that

I'm after; they owe someone money.' Thank goodness she'd remembered their name on the entry system.

Venus noticed the boy easing his fighting stance a little.

'Who do they owe money to?' he asked.

Venus desperately thought on her feet. 'The guy I work for lent them a big sum. They didn't pay it back. My job is to get something – anything.'

'How do we know you're telling the truth?' said the girl, scowling.

'When you came in I was on my way out. I told you, I've got no interest in your flat – it's just my entry point.'

The boy lowered his fists a few centimetres and looked round at the girl.

'How did you get in then?' asked the girl.

'I used the scaffolding,' replied Venus.

'What, you jumped from the scaffolding on number 36?' asked the boy with shock.

'No, I swung on to your flat roof with the help of the masonry at number 34. Now are we finished in here? I have work to do.'

Venus could see that both of them were impressed with how she'd broken in.

'And you weren't sent to get anything from us?' asked the girl.

Interesting, thought Venus. *They must be involved in*

something dodgy – they're not so much cross that I'm here as worried that I may be after them!

Venus raised her eyes to the heavens. 'How many times do I have to tell you? I don't know who you are. I don't care about you.'

Venus kept her body taut, ready for a fight, but inside she relaxed a little. She realised they weren't going to call the police. In fact, they seemed to believe her story.

'You swung from the scaffolding,' the boy stated. 'That was pretty risky. There must have been an easier way to get into that flat.'

Venus said nothing.

'You must know what you're doing to get in that way,' the boy continued. He swallowed deeply. 'What's your name?'

'Kerry,' replied Venus. She'd thought it sounded good when she was planning her possible cover stories.

'OK, Kerry,' he went on. 'Well I've got some bad news for you. I have to tell you that the Wiltons moved out three weeks ago. They've rented the place. They took all of their own stuff with them, so if you're after payback you can forget it – they're not there.'

Venus pretended to look cross but was pleased that they obviously believed her story.

The boy looked across at the girl, who glared back at him.

'Who are you working for?' asked the boy. 'Who sent you in?'

'None of your business. Anyway, it was a one-off,' replied Venus. 'If there's nothing down there I'm out of here.'

'What will the guy do when he finds out the Wiltons have gone?' asked the boy.

Venus shrugged her shoulders. 'Don't know. He'll get someone else to track them down. If he hasn't even managed to get his facts right, I'm not interested in working for him any more.'

No one said anything for a few seconds.

'Would you be interested in some . . . some other work?' the boy asked.

Of all the things Venus had expected him to say, it certainly wasn't this. Part of her was horrified – what danger would it involve? But another part of her felt that she was being offered an opportunity which may well lead her to Franco and provide her with the evidence Radcliff needed.

'It better not be like tonight,' said Venus harshly. 'No Wiltons means no cash for me.'

'How do you know we can trust her, Paul?' snapped the girl.

'Leave it, Mel. I know what I'm doing,' he answered.

'Can you just get on with this?' said Venus irritably, although inside her heart was thudding with excitement; this was looking promising.

'Look,' said Paul, 'we've got a job on tomorrow. It's a job that could well lead to other jobs. We could do with someone who's agile and can think on their feet.' Venus recalled hearing the conversation about a three person job.

'This is stupid,' hissed Mel. 'We don't know her.'

Paul ignored her and stayed focussed on Venus. 'Would you be up for it? If it all works out you'll be rewarded well.'

Venus pretended to think the matter over for a moment.

'What kind of job is it?' she demanded.

Paul frowned. 'I'm not going to tell you now – you might be anyone; you could go blabbing to the police.'

'What, after I just broke in here?' Venus asked, an incredulous expression on her face.

'OK, OK.' Paul nodded. 'This is the way I see it. We'll let you go. I'm taking a massive gamble on you but I think it might be worth it. Tomorrow afternoon at five forty-five, meet us on the corner of Adams Street and Turner Avenue – you know, behind the multiplex cinema?'

Venus nodded. 'How do I know you're not setting me up?'

'You don't,' he replied. 'Just show up and help us tomorrow. If you're prepared to hang around for a few days, I'll make sure you get a decent stash.'

'I'll think about it,' replied Venus.

Paul stared at her and she stared back.

'Well?' asked Paul.

'I said I'll think about it,' answered Venus, 'and it would make my life much easier if you told me what the job was.'

Paul sighed. 'Franco only tells us at the last minute. He lets us know the meeting place and the time and then explains the job just before it kicks off.'

Franco! Even though she'd heard him with Mel and Paul earlier, the mention of his name made Venus go cold.

'Who is *Franco*?' asked Venus trying to keep her voice calm and regular.

'None of your business,' said Mel.

'Will he be there?' asked Venus.

Paul shook his head. Mel said nothing.

Venus blew her cheeks out. 'OK,' she said. 'Can I go now?'

'OK,' agreed Paul. 'But be there tomorrow afternoon.'

'We'll see,' replied Venus.

The next moment she was being led down two long flights of stairs, passing the first floor flat and the Wiltons' property on the ground floor as Mel unlocked the big front door. She stood to one side shaking her head.

'I don't trust you,' she hissed at Venus.

Venus barged past her, bumping her with her shoulder.

'The feeling's mutual,' Venus replied.

'Five forty-five p.m. tomorrow,' said Paul.

Venus didn't reply. She pulled her jacket tighter and hurried off into the night. She could barely believe her luck – she had found out far more than she'd hoped. But she couldn't ignore the chill of one persistent thought – what was she getting herself into?

Chapter Four

'How was it, hon?'

Gail Spring was just coming downstairs when her daughter returned home.

I swung on some scaffolding, broke into a flat and got taken on for some kind of dodgy assignment tomorrow.

'It was good,' Venus responded.

'What was it called?'

'*Purple Night*,' replied Venus a little too enthusiastically. 'It had Saffron Ritchie in.' She'd made sure she'd read a short review and summary of the film on the internet.

'She's pretty good, isn't she?' said Gail.

'Yeah,' nodded Venus with a sigh of relief.

Gail reached the bottom of the stairs as Venus closed the front door.

'Look,' Gail began, 'I've been thinking. Things have

been very tense round here and it hasn't been helped because I'm so busy at work. How about we go out for a meal one night. You know – have a chance for a proper chat, sort things out?'

'Sure,' smiled Venus, 'good idea.'

Her mum squeezed her elbow. 'Great,' she replied, 'I'll book somewhere.'

Gail then went to the kitchen and Venus headed to her room, her mind whirring.

The following day, Venus found it almost impossible to concentrate at school. Mr Reece, her geography teacher, asked her if she was dreaming about the Christmas holidays. Mrs Tyler, her science teacher, instructed Venus to focus several times. But lessons didn't feel important at all. She was meeting Paul and Mel in a few hours and she had no idea what would happen next.

Franco wasn't going to be there – at least that's what Paul seemed to think. Presumably he told them the job specifics by mobile phone. But what if he changed his mind and turned up? He'd recognise her instantly. And what if Paul told Franco about this amazingly agile girl who'd broken into his flat? Might Franco guess it was her? Thank goodness she'd been wearing her hair tucked up in her beanie hat. Her long dark hair was the most distinctive thing about her.

'Hey, Venus.'

Venus was in the canteen sipping from a can of Coke when Kate approached her table and sat down. 'Come over after school,' she said. 'I've got some great new music you'll love.'

Venus was suddenly overcome by an urge to tell Kate about Paul and Mel and the job this afternoon, but she held back. She knew her secret would be safe with Kate but Kate would probably freak out and launch a one-woman campaign to stop her. She'd told her about trying to follow Franco the day before when Kate had phoned to quiz her about how she'd ended up in an unknown street – but she'd explained it was just a wild goose chase.

'Can't,' replied Venus, 'got stuff to do.'

'Like what?'

'Got to pop round to Dennis's place.'

Kate pulled a face. 'Er, Dennis is in Peru,' she pointed out.

'I know, but I've got some things at his flat that I need.'

Kate fixed her best mate with a hard stare. 'What's going on, Venus?' she asked. 'You seem really distracted. Has something new happened with the Franco situation?'

'No,' replied Venus firmly, 'it's just things with Mum.'

'Still not good?' asked Kate sympathetically.

Venus shook her head. 'But she's offered to take me out for a meal and talk things over – I think she wants to patch things up.'

'Sounds good,' nodded Kate. 'Why don't you come over after you've been to Dennis's?'

Venus smiled weakly. 'Not tonight, Kate. Can we do it tomorrow?'

The rest of the day dragged and it seemed like a hundred hours had passed by the time the last lesson finished at four p.m. It would take about half an hour to cycle to the meeting place.

I want to get there early. That way I'll have the chance to position myself out of sight and stake it out; see if Franco turns up. If he does, I won't.

Venus got to the school's IT centre with half an hour to kill. She browsed the internet for a while and checked out the website for *The Dust Deceiver* – a new Hollywood film that boasted Kelly Tanner as its main stunt artist. But she didn't really focus on anything she read – her mind was on the following few hours. Gail had told her that she wouldn't be back until after nine tonight. Venus hoped *she'd* be back well before then. If she wasn't – well, she'd cross that bridge when she came to it.

At four forty-five, Venus went outside, slipping on

her beanie hat and scarf. She unlocked her bike from the rack at the back of the science block and sped off. Half an hour later she cycled to the top of Turner Avenue and turned into a side road. It was now five-fifteen – thirty minutes until the meeting time.

Venus locked her bike against a lamppost. She clenched and unclenched her fists; now she was here she felt really apprehensive.

Please don't let this job be violent.

Luckily there was a café nearby where she had a perfect view of the meeting place. She bought a paper in the newsagents next door, then sat down at one of the outdoor tables and ordered a cappuccino.

Venus felt like a spy in some old French film; she held the paper up and angled it so that she could constantly look at the corner without attracting any attention.

At five-forty, Venus saw Paul and Mel approach the corner. They were locked in intense conversation and Paul was carrying a black briefcase. Venus felt an immense sweep of relief as she realised Franco wasn't with them.

A few minutes later and Franco still hadn't turned up. Thank goodness! Venus checked that Paul and Mel weren't looking her way, put the paper down and walked straight down the street towards them.

'So you made it?' said Paul, as Venus reached them.

Mel muttered something under her breath, but Paul shook his head irritably. 'Cut it out,' he said, eyeing her angrily. 'We've got a job to do and we're going to do it. Don't forget why we're here; we're going to make a sizeable pile of cash in the next few days if we do things properly. If we don't work together this whole thing will fall apart, got it?'

Venus nodded. Mel didn't respond to this troop-rousing speech.

'OK,' said Venus, 'I'm here. Now are you going to tell me what we're going to do?'

Paul pulled out his mobile from his trouser pocket and punched in a number quickly.

'It's me,' he said when the call was answered. The following three-minute conversation consisted of him listening almost the whole time and uttering the occasional 'Yes', or 'Got it'.

As soon as the call was finished he turned to Venus and Mel. 'OK,' he said, 'here's what Franco said.'

This is ultra weird. I'm part of a gang that takes its orders from Franco Dane.

Venus tried to ignore her thoughts and leaned in towards him to listen intently.

'Ten shops down, there's an Indian restaurant called The Sun Sage,' Paul informed them. 'A man who works in an office near here goes to that restaurant *every* Tuesday and Thursday without fail, from six p.m. to seven for their 'Early Bird' supper. He always sits at the table nearest the radiator on the left hand side of the restaurant. And he always carries a black briefcase, exactly like this one – which Franco gave me this morning.

'What we need is some information – which is in his briefcase,' Paul went on. 'It's absolutely vital that he knows nothing of our activities. If he realises this information has been stolen, he'll up his security, which will make our next job virtually impossible. So, this is the plan. We wait until just after six, then the two of you go into the restaurant and sit at the table on the other side of the room, the one parallel to his table. You then order some food.'

Sit at a table with Mel and look like we're just hanging out? That's not going to be much fun! She detests me.

'This guy absolutely loves his food,' said Paul. 'A couple of minutes after the waiter starts bringing him dishes, I want you, Mel, to text me. I'll then come into the restaurant and walk down the aisle towards his table. When I get near him, one of you will need to distract him. At that second I'll switch his briefcase for this one. I'll then come over to your table for a brief chat and tell you loudly that I've got a couple of things to do and that I'll be back in ten minutes.'

Venus nodded, taking in every word.

'There's a photocopier in the newsagent round the corner. I'll photocopy the documents we need and then come back into the restaurant.'

'Is this some cheesy 1970s spy film?' asked Venus with a wry smile.

Paul smiled. Mel didn't.

'Will it be as easy as that?' asked Venus. 'Won't the briefcase be locked?'

'Anyone can pick a lock like that,' replied Mel.

Venus felt Mel was purposefully trying to squash her.

'I'll pass his table again,' Paul continued, 'and swap the briefcases back. Keep a careful look out – you may need to distract him again. I'll then walk over to you two and sit down at the table. At seven the guy will pay his bill and go, leaving us at our table. He will have absolutely no idea what's just happened and he'll go home with a full belly and as far as he's concerned, an untouched briefcase. That's it.'

'Why does *she* need to be here?' demanded Mel sulkily.

'It's easier for two people to create a distraction. We always intended this to be a three man job – you know that.'

Mel shrugged her shoulders sulkily.

They hung back and stood outside a closed leather goods store. Sure enough, just before six p.m. a large, overweight, bald man in a grey mac, carrying a black briefcase by his side, stepped inside The Sun Sage.

Paul checked his watch and the three of them waited.

'OK,' nodded Paul after two minutes. 'Go.'

Venus and Mel started walking down the street.

'Look,' said Venus, 'we need to be civil to each other in there. We'll only draw attention to ourselves if we just sit glaring at each other.'

'Whatever, just leave it to me. I'll do the distracting bit,' said Mel sharply. 'And I don't need any help; got it?'

'Fine,' replied Venus testily.

They reached the front door of The Sun Sage and stepped inside. The place had red carpet, mirrors on the walls and Indian artefacts on the ceiling. Venus counted fifteen tables. The bald man was sitting at his regular table on the left; Franco's research was good.

Just as he'd instructed, Venus and Mel walked over to the parallel table at the other side of the room, sat down and checked out the menus.

'I don't even like Indian food,' muttered Mel.

'Surely there's something you like,' Venus replied a tad impatiently.

Venus stole a glance at the bald guy. He was talking to a waiter who was writing his order down on a notepad. The waiter said something to the man, they both laughed and then the waiter disappeared into the kitchens. He appeared a minute later and came over to Venus's table.

'Evening, ladies, what can I get you?'

'I'll have the vegetable korma and some naan bread please,' said Venus.

'I'll have the same,' added Mel.

OK, this is my chance to find out a bit about Mel, Paul and especially Franco, thought Venus.

'How old are you two?' enquired Venus, when the waiter had retreated.

'I'm sixteen, Paul's seventeen,' replied Mel, looking around the otherwise empty restaurant.

'How long have you known him?'

'About three years.'

'And are you two . . . ?'

'No,' replied Mel quickly. 'The flat is just a convenience thing. Franco sorted it out.'

'This Franco guy sounds like a bit of a mover and shaker,' observed Venus.

'Yeah,' nodded Mel, 'but he's living in his own world a bit at the moment.'

Venus bristled. 'What do you mean?'

But Mel's attention was diverted. The waiter had just

reappeared carrying a tray full of small dishes for the bald man.

'Sorry,' said Venus, desperate to steer the conversation back to her chosen subject, 'what were you saying about Franco?'

'Stop asking questions,' hissed Mel. 'Let's just do this thing and get out of here.'

The man started tucking into his dishes and Mel texted Paul, as instructed.

A minute later the door of The Sun Sage swung open and Paul came in, carrying his own case. Mel quickly stood up and walked towards the man's table.

'Excuse me, have you got a light?' she asked, pulling a cigarette out of her jacket pocket.

The man looked up reluctantly from his meal and eyed Mel. As he did this, Paul reached the table and made the switch in one swift, smooth movement. He then strolled over to where Venus was sitting.

'Er, I don't smoke,' the man told Mel firmly, 'and anyway it's illegal to smoke inside a restaurant. Didn't you know that?'

'I was going to have it outside,' Mel explained, 'but it doesn't matter. I'll have one later. Sorry to trouble you.'

So she does have a tiny bit of politeness in her body.

Mel returned to the table and sat down opposite Venus. Paul remained standing.

'Sorry I'm late,' he said loudly, 'but I've got a couple of things to do. Will you still be here in ten minutes?'

'Sure,' replied Mel, 'of course we'll be here.'

Venus saw Paul's right hand gripping the briefcase handle tightly.

'OK,' he smiled, 'see you in a bit.'

A few minutes later, the waiter appeared carrying their kormas on a tray along with two gigantic lengths of naan bread and they started to eat. Mel picked at her food, but after a few mouthfuls Venus could see that she was actually beginning to enjoy it.

'Are you into music?' asked Venus, dipping a piece of naan bread into the smooth, coconut sauce of the korma.

'I like R 'n' B,' replied Mel curtly.

Their stilted conversation was eventually interrupted by the loud ring tone of the bald man's phone. Venus stole a glance over at him.

'Really?' his voice boomed. 'Are you sure about that?'

Venus looked at Mel, who was toying with piece of naan bread.

'Well if there's no other way, I'll come over for it. I'll be there in about ten minutes.'

He shook his head and ended the call.

Venus checked her watch. It was only six-thirty. If he was going to be somewhere in ten minutes he'd have to leave here before that ten minutes was up. His six until seven routine would be broken. Venus glanced anxiously at the door; there was no sign of Paul.

'Text Paul,' hissed Venus.

Mel did this instantly.

A few uncomfortable minutes passed. It was now 6.33 p.m.

'Any reply?' asked Venus.

Mel shook her head.

'What are we going to do?' asked Venus.

'We sit and wait,' replied Mel uneasily.

So they sat and waited.

6.35 p.m. passed. The bald guy didn't move, but there was still no sign of Paul.

'Text him again,' said Venus.

Mel tapped her phone keys furiously.

At 6.37 p.m., the man waved to the waiter and asked for the bill. Venus gripped the table anxiously. *Come on, Paul. Where the hell are you? You said the man mustn't know that his briefcase has been touched, but at this rate, he'll find out that the damn thing's been stolen!*

Mel was looking ultra anxious too.

The waiter appeared with the bill on a small silver tray and the man reached into his pocket and dug out his wallet. Venus checked the door again.

6.39 p.m.

There was still no sign of Paul.

Mel was biting her bottom lip.

The bald man stood up.

I've got to do something to salvage this.

Venus stood up quickly and made a beeline for the other side of the restaurant.

'Keep the change,' the man said to the waiter, reaching for his coat on the back of his chair. 'Something's come up. I'll see you tomorrow.'

The waiter thanked him, took the money and went away.

Venus reached a spot just behind the bald man. She walked forward a couple of steps and then stumbled, yelped in surprise and fell forward. She flung out her arms dramatically and grabbed the edge of the man's table in her best Kelly Tanner, stunt-girl move. All of those times diving through sugar glass on film sets had stood her in good stead for pulling off such a feat.

With a blur of movement and a cacophony of noise, she pulled the table over with her as she smashed onto the floor. As she hit the carpet, bowls and plates and cutlery crashed to the ground, landing on or beside Venus. As Venus tumbled, she spotted Paul sliding through the restaurant door and hurrying towards them. As he drew up close he switched the briefcases back in a flash.

The waiter alerted by the noise, ran out of the kitchen.

'Are you OK?' asked the bald man leaning over her.

Paul was already halfway across the room towards Mel.

'Er, I'm fine. I'm getting these dizzy spells, but I'm OK now,' replied Venus. 'Sorry about the mess.'

'Don't worry,' smiled the waiter kindly, 'these things happen.'

Venus sat up and brushed some popadom crumbs from her hair.

'Look, I have to leave,' announced the bald man. 'Are you sure you're OK?'

'I'm fine, thanks,' smiled Venus, standing up and helping the waiter pick up the table.

The bald man nodded in a businesslike fashion and reached down for his briefcase. 'Right then,' he said, turning to the waiter. 'I'll see you very soon.'

The waiter smiled and the man left.

Venus and the waiter finished straightening the table and the waiter busied himself with picking things up off the floor. Venus strolled back to her own table. where Paul was putting down money for the bill. Mel didn't make eye contact with her as she approached, but Paul looked at her with respect.

'What took you so long?' asked Venus, sitting down and polishing off a piece of naan bread.

'I thought I had plenty of time, but the photocopier took ages to get started,' Paul explained. 'When it got going it was OK, but I can't believe he left early.'

'It's just one of those things,' remarked Venus. 'Probably some crisis at work.'

'Well, the table throwing worked a treat,' smiled Paul. 'Don't you reckon, Mel?'

Mel shrugged. 'S'pose so.'

'So we got what we wanted, yeah?' asked Venus as they left the restaurant, 'What happens next?'

'I told you earlier,' Paul reminded her, 'Franco never tells us anything in advance. He'll let us know at the last minute.'

Venus shook her head. 'Seems like a mad way to work,' she remarked.

'What would you know?' sneered Mel.

'Leave it out, Mel!' hissed Paul. 'Without Kerry this job would have gone badly wrong. I didn't see you on your feet back there.'

'Look, I've got to go,' said Mel to Paul. 'I'll see you back at the flat.' And with that she crossed the road and disappeared into a side street.

'This Franco guy, he's very elusive, isn't he?' said Venus trying to be casual as she and Paul walked on.

'He's a bit of a loner,' replied Paul, 'but he's excellent at what he does.'

'Is he going to be joining us for the next job?' asked Venus.

'No,' replied Paul, 'he'll set it all up and the three of us will do it.'

'What – so you run the risk of getting caught and he gets the prize?'

'It's not like that,' replied Paul. 'He's just got some personal stuff to sort out.'

'Did you tell Franco I'd be on this job?'

'Of course,' replied Paul.

'What did you tell him?'

Paul glanced at her sideways. 'I said I'd found someone to help out. Why?'

'No reason,' said Venus.

'He wanted my assurance that you'd be OK,' added Paul.

'How could you tell him I'd be OK when you've only just met me?'

For a second Venus was sure she saw the trace of a blush on Paul's cheeks.

'You didn't tell him that you'd only just met me, did you?' she said. 'You let him assume you'd known me for ages and that you knew I was totally reliable?'

Paul's cheeks remained a faint shade of red. It suddenly dawned on Venus that Paul rather liked her. Well, she could use that to her advantage, couldn't she?

She also realised with relief, that that was why probably why Mel objected to her so much; she was jealous.

'Look,' said Paul. 'I've got to shoot. Give me your mobile number.'

Venus hesitated a second.

'I won't give it to anyone else,' promised Paul, 'if that's what you're worried about.'

'No, it's cool,' replied Venus, hoping she sounded confident about this.

She gave Paul her number and he entered it into his phone

'I'll be in touch,' he said, tucking his phone back into his trouser pocket. 'I need to give you your cut. And I want you to stay involved.'

'I don't think Mel feels that way,' Venus pointed out.

Paul took a deep breath and blew the air out slowly. 'Mel is . . . how can I put this . . . not the most positive of people. She's had a hard time and she's very cynical, but she's very reliable. It just takes her ages to trust people.'

'It doesn't look like she'll *ever* trust me.'

'She saw what you did today. She'll accept you – just give it a while.'

'OK,' agreed Venus, 'but I'm not convinced.'

Paul checked his watch. 'Look, Kerry, I've got to go and get these things. I'll call you. You were great today.'

Venus couldn't help but be pleased by Paul's praise and was shocked at herself; this was the first time she'd ever assisted a crime.

'Fine,' replied Venus. 'See you.'

Paul crossed the road and disappeared into an electrical store.

As Venus hurried off to get her bike, she glanced quickly over her shoulder a couple of times, just in case Paul was on her tail. As Venus walked, the cogs in her brain worked furiously.

What did Paul photocopy? And what will the next job be?

It was seven-thirty by the time Venus got home. There was a message from her mum on the answerphone: 'Hi, hon, it's me. I have to finish up a couple of things and I'll be back later than nine – not too much. But I've booked us a table at a nice restaurant the day after tomorrow. We can have a good chat then, OK? Hopefully see you later. Sleep well.'

Venus opened the fridge door, thinking about Gail. As always her mum was working far too hard. She knew that Gail was very committed to her career as a barrister, but whatever happened to the work/life balance? Gail hardly allowed herself any leisure time – it was ridiculous. Venus resolved to talk to her mum about it over their meal. Venus missed just spending time with her mum. She sometimes felt that Gail was less interested in Venus than her work, although in her heart she knew that wasn't true. Still, she felt shut out from Gail's life. But as she picked out a yogurt and sat down at the empty kitchen table, Venus realised with a start that she was doing exactly the same. While she didn't want to worry her mum about her stunt life, by not telling her anything about it, it was like keeping her mum from knowing the real her. Venus thought about the day's activities – Mel, Paul, the briefcase, Franco . . . No, she couldn't tell Gail anything yet. She needed to stop Franco from whatever he was up to. Some secrets would have to be kept a while longer.

Chapter Five

Two days later, Venus was hanging out with Kate near the school canteen, when a younger boy approached her nervously. 'Are you Venus Sting?' he asked.

'It's *Spring*,' answered Venus, 'and yes that's me.'

'Well, some boy at the school gates gave me this and asked me to give it to you; it's taken me ages to find you.'

Venus felt her body shaking as the old fear crept over her. The boy passed her a white envelope. There was no writing on the front.

'What did he look like?' demanded Venus.

'I dunno really,' the boy replied. 'He was tall with brown hair. I only saw him for a second.'

'OK.' Venus nodded. 'Thanks for bringing it to me.'

The boy shrugged his shoulders and hurried away. Venus and Kate exchanged anxious looks. Venus opened the envelope. Inside was a single sheet of white paper. She stared at the words, written in black ink, in that all-too-familiar style.

You can't see me, but I can see you.

'What is it?' asked Kate.

Despite her plan, Venus found she was trembling and her hands were suddenly sticky. She had to sit down and, as she did so, she handed her friend the note. Kate gulped nervously as she stared at the piece of paper. 'You know what, Venus, I think I might have been wrong about Franco. Maybe he *is* stalking you. From everything you've told me about his past behaviour, maybe you're not safe.'

'But what can I do?' asked Venus. She'd told Kate all about her meeting with DCI Radcliff at the British Museum.

'Well, if these notes aren't enough for Radcliff, why don't you show them to the head teacher?' suggested Kate. 'Maybe there's something she could do?'

Venus shook her head. 'She'd probably just call the police and we'd be back to square one. They've got better things to do – they'd just see it as a school issue.'

'I don't agree,' said Kate with a deep frown. 'We know Franco is a bit of a psycho. Maybe the police could do surveillance or something and catch him the next time he appears. You don't have to go to Radcliff, you could just go to the local police.'

Venus thought back to her clashes with Franco at stunt camp. He'd repeatedly driven a motorbike straight at the phone box she was in and she'd only just managed to escape, with the help of a ferocious kick to the door. And then there was the face-off in the log barn – he'd advanced on her with that evil expression on his face that sent shivers down her spine. Thank goodness she'd acted quickly and started an avalanche of logs that fell onto him. She was terrified of Franco – completely terrified. She knew he would think nothing of killing her.

'No, Kate,' said Venus, returning to the present. 'The police won't set up an observation on the school all day, every day – it just won't happen.'

'How do you know? Stalking is a serious crime. You see it in the papers all the time. These people need to be put away.'

'I agree, but as Radcliff said, there's no clear evidence,' said Venus, folding the note and putting it into her jacket pocket. 'I just need to wait a bit.'

Kate's expression suddenly hardened. 'Oh my God, Venus,' she hissed. 'You're not planning something ridiculously dangerous are you? I know what you're like.'

'No way.' Venus smiled. 'I'm just going to bide my time and nail him when the moment is right.'

'Well you're not walking to and from school by yourself any more. I'm coming with you on both journeys, every day.'

'I'm not a baby,' protested Venus. 'I don't need my hand held; I can look after myself.'

'I'm not saying you can't, but he's far less likely to do anything if someone else is with you.'

Venus sighed. 'OK, you win; we'll do all of the journeys together – except when I can't.'

'When will that happen?' asked Kate suspiciously.

'It doesn't matter; anyway, aren't you going on a run after school?'

'I'll miss it so that we can walk home together.'

'Stick with the run,' replied Venus. 'I'll be fine, honestly.'

Kate arched an eyebrow. 'I've heard that one before,' she said in an accusing tone, 'and you've had a few too many close calls . . . Luck runs out, you know, Venus.'

'Stop worrying,' commanded Venus. 'There's no immediate danger.'

But the truth was, anxiety pressed heavily on her. Yes, she'd defeated Franco before, but this time she might not be so lucky. And it definitely seemed like he was out to get her somehow.

The restaurant Gail Spring chose for the meal with her daughter was called The Tuscan Table, an Italian place just off Islington High Street. Gail had promised to take her so many times and always cancelled, so Venus was amazed to actually find herself there. They'd just finished two pieces of mouth-watering garlic bread.

'How was school?' asked Gail.

'The usual,' replied Venus, 'a bit of English, a bit of maths, a bit of geography, you know how it is. How was your day? I bet it was a million times more interesting.'

'A bit of court, a bit of meetings, a bit of hassled phone conversations, you know how it is.'

There was silence for a few seconds, then they both laughed. It was the first time they'd laughed for ages. At that moment the waitress appeared with two bowls of piping hot pasta and laid them carefully on the table.

Gail took a sip from her glass of red wine. 'I'm a bit concerned about you at the minute, Venus,' she began. 'You look a bit drawn – a bit down.'

Venus picked up her fork. 'There's just loads of coursework to do at school,' she replied.

'Is there anything I can help you with?'

'Nah, it's fine; I've just finished a big English project so things will slack off for a bit.'

'Good.' Gail smiled.

They both tucked into their food.

'I've been doing a lot of thinking about your father,' said Gail after a couple of minutes.

Venus pushed her fork in a circle. She'd been so distracted with the whole Franco thing recently that she had hardly given Elliot a thought.

'What now?' she asked.

Gail pursed her lips and managed a weak smile. 'Venus; I haven't come here to argue; in fact quite the opposite.'

Venus let go of her fork.

'I'm still upset and angry that you stayed in contact with him without telling me, but I've started trying to put myself in your shoes.'

Venus stared at her mother, fascinated to hear what was coming next.

'And that's really helped me. I can see why you did it and I've decided that I can live with it. I'm not going to have a big reconciliation with him but it's fine for you to speak to him and see him.'

Venus felt tears of relief snaking down her cheeks. This was a very big concession from Gail and she knew it. She dried her eyes with a napkin. 'You mean it, don't you?'

Gail nodded. Her eyes were watery too.

'I'm really, really sorry I didn't tell you about meeting him,' said Venus, 'but I knew you'd go crazy if you found out. I know you'd totally blocked him out of your life and never wanted me to see him, but when the opportunity arose, I had to take it.'

'I understand,' replied Gail softly, 'and there's no way I'm going to let this thing ruin our lives. We're a good team aren't we?'

'Totally.' Venus grinned. 'Always have been, always will be!'

'So no more secrets from now on?' said Gail.

Venus gave a smile, hoping it looked genuine, and took another mouthful of pasta.

Venus's mobile went at morning break in school the next Monday.

Private number, read the display.

'Hello?'

'It's Paul. Can you talk?'

For a second Venus couldn't think of any Paul she knew, but then she suddenly realised who it was.

Venus nodded to the girls she'd been chatting to and walked away from them, down the corridor to the end of the lockers where no one was around.

'I can talk now,' she said.

'I want to meet you tonight to discuss something.

Can you do the café on Drayton Bridge at eight?'

'I suppose so.'

'Good. I'll meet you then.' The line went dead.

Venus cursed herself for not asking if Franco would be there. She tucked away her phone and crossed her fingers that he wouldn't show.

Paul was already in the café, reading a newspaper, when Venus arrived. She was feeling nervous, her eyes flitting in different directions, looking for a sign of Franco. She sat down opposite him, in a corner booth. Steam swirled into the air from an urn on the counter and the aroma of coffee beans mixed with the tantalising smell of cakes and pastries.

Once she'd got a coffee, Paul began. 'OK, this is how things stand. Franco's looked over the documents we photocopied and he says they're just what we need for the next job.'

'When's that going to be?'

'This Saturday,' replied Paul. 'I want you involved again. There'll be a lot more of this if you agree to do it. Are you up for it?'

He slid a small wad of ten-pound notes across the table. Venus reckoned there must be at least a hundred pounds there.

'I'll think about it,' replied Venus, curling her right

hand round the notes. 'Will this Franco guy be there this time?' she asked.

'I'm not sure. To be honest, he's been acting a bit strangely recently. He told me he's got some sort of vendetta against someone – sounded like one of those mafia jobs.'

Venus felt her throat constrict and her palms go clammy.

'Did he say who this vendetta is against?' she asked.

'No, he's a very secretive guy.'

'Not even a clue?'

Paul shook his head and changed the subject. 'So are you up for it?'

'It depends what it is,' replied Venus.

'Franco will only tell me at the last minute – just like all the other jobs.'

Paul's mouth suddenly dropped open and he looked very nervous. 'Don't look round,' he whispered 'and hide that money now.'

Venus was desperate to look behind her, but she didn't. Instead, she tucked the cash into her jacket pocket.

'In twenty seconds we're going to get up and leave, really casually, OK?' Paul whispered.

'What's up?' hissed Venus.

'You'll see in a minute.'

Out of the corner of her eye Venus spotted two police officers standing at the counter and talking in hushed tones to the café's owner.

'Come on,' said Paul.

As soon as they stood up, one of the policemen headed straight in their direction and fixed them with an intent stare.

Venus thought her heart might stop at any second.

'Have you finished with that newspaper?' he asked, nodding to the one Paul had left on the table.

Venus was so tense she almost screamed with relief, but instead she picked up the paper from the table and handed it over, hoping that he didn't notice her shaking hand.

'Cheers.' The officer nodded, then walked back over to his colleague. Venus and Paul headed to the door and stepped out into the cold night. They both stole a quick glance back at the café to make sure the policemen hadn't followed them, but the coast was clear.

Venus's head was spinning with one word: *vendetta*.

'I'm taking the bus to town,' said Paul.

'I'm going the other way,' said Venus. 'Where are we meeting on Saturday?'

Paul pulled his jacket tighter against the wind. 'I'll call you,' he replied.

Venus nodded goodbye and they headed off in separate directions.

During the days that followed, Venus was completely preoccupied. It was one thing wondering what Franco would do, but quite another to hear Paul talk about an actual vendetta. She was certain that this personal vendetta was against her – the timing with the notes proved it. If so, she was in very real danger. She was desperate to contact DCI Radcliff, but once again she felt she didn't have the proof that Radcliff needed. If only her father was around – or Dennis. She knew she could always phone them, but she didn't see the point. How could they help her from hundreds of miles away?

Venus slept in on Saturday morning. At midday, her mobile on the bedside table went, waking her.

'It's Paul.'

Venus wiped the sleep out of her eyes and sat up.

'It's about tonight.'

Venus suddenly felt nervous energy powering her body. 'Where are we meeting?'

'Do you know Willow Street? It's round the back of that theatre – that one with the really tacky model bear on its roof. Near the river?'

'I know it,' said Venus.

'OK, there's a road behind the theatre's car park, called Anderson Avenue. Go down that and near the end on your right is an opening to a narrow lane. It's called Fisherman's Way. Go to the end and we'll meet you there.'

'You mean you and Mel?'

'Yep.'

'Is she still giving you grief for including me in this set up?'

'It doesn't matter. We need you.'

'What time are we meeting?'

'Three a.m.'

Venus gulped.

'Is that a problem?' asked Paul.

'Er, no, it's fine,' replied Venus. 'I'll be there. And has Franco given you any idea what we're after?'

'I told you, he's Mr Last Minute. He'll call me later with instructions. Will you be there?'

'I'll be there,' replied Venus.

'Good,' said Paul, wrapping up the call, 'I'll see you later.'

'Mum,' said Venus, padding into Gail's office. 'There's a whole load of people going to a party tonight and Heidi said I can crash at hers.'

Gail pulled a face. 'Where does she live?'

Venus told her, and was forced to go into far more detail than she wanted to about whose party it was, who was going to be there, and how long it was going to last.

Gail took a deep breath. 'OK Venus, but I want her mum's phone number.'

Venus wrote down the number in Gail's diary but she transposed the last two digits; if her mum did try to use it, she'd pretend it was a mistake.

'I'll cook lunch,' said Venus brightly, 'I'll do those veggie pancakes – the ones from that American cookbook you got for your birthday. You know, the one you've *never opened*!'

Gail smiled. 'I've just got this speech for court to finish.'

'Come down in twenty minutes,' said Venus, 'and all will be ready.'

'Thanks, Venus.' Gail nodded appreciatively. 'It's a date.'

Venus made lunch as light an affair as possible. She talked about school and told Gail stories about the teachers and their particular foibles. She reminisced about their summer holiday in France, the one they'd had after stunt camp. It wasn't just for Gail's benefit – it was for hers too; it helped take her mind off the enormous challenges and risks that the coming hours might bring.

After lunch, she reluctantly did some English homework – the start of an essay about Shakespeare's *Othello*. She then lay on the sofa listening to her iPod and reading a thriller set in New York. At seven p.m. she ate supper with her mum, watched a bit of some rubbish reality show on TV and then went back to her bedroom. She put on her black jeans, a long-sleeved black T-shirt and a black hooded sweatshirt. In the pockets of this she put a twenty pound note, a small pencil torch, her train pass, her keys and her mobile. At eight-thirty p.m. she emerged from her room.

Gail was downstairs sitting at the kitchen table marking up some legal documents.

'Mum, give work a rest,' implored Venus more in hope than expectation.

'Don't worry – I'll be finished in half an hour. I'm meeting Suzie and Monique for a drink later. We'll be at The Oyster Bar round the corner. I'll have my phone on so give me a ring at any time.'

'Sure.' Venus smiled, stooping down to give her a kiss on the cheek.

'Are you going for that film noir look tonight?' asked Gail, observing her daughter's wholly black outfit.

'Something like that,' grinned Venus. 'We'll head to the party and then go back to Heidi's. We'll be shattered so I probably won't come back till lunchtime tomorrow or later.

That gives me the biggest possible time frame.

'I'll give you a bell when I wake up.'

'You do that,' said Gail firmly. 'You might have to ring my mobile though – I'm out tomorrow morning.'

Venus flashed her mum a smile and then left the house.

Chapter Six

Venus caught a bus and it was 9.05 p.m. when she got into town. She'd had very strong urges to call DCI Radcliff during the day; tonight's job sounded far more like a serious crime than the briefcase switch. But she'd resisted. She needed to wait and only go to Radcliff when she had some concrete information.

With just under six hours to kill, Venus headed straight to the multiplex cinema where they were showing the new Saffron Ritchie film, *Purple Night*. She'd lied to her mum about seeing it before, but it had sounded pretty good in the reviews. The programme started at ten p.m. The film was billed as a thriller, but Venus didn't find it very thrilling – partly because she found it almost impossible to concentrate. However, it was long, which was useful.

When it had finished, she hurried down the street

and into Al's café, which stayed open all night. She ordered a cappuccino and a biscotti and read every magazine in the place. She'd always looked old for her age and could easily pass for eighteen, but she still felt edgy being a single female around town in the early hours. Luckily no one bothered her.

When she'd finished her third cappuccino she checked the large clock on the café wall. 2.40 a.m.; time to make a move. As she walked round the back of the multiplex, her eyes darted this way and that.

Paul's directions were excellent and ten minutes later she found herself stepping into Fisherman's Way. It was lit by one small lamppost and she hurried down it. When she emerged at the other end, she found herself on a rectangle of concrete about twenty metres square, right beside the River Thames. Ahead of her was a large dinghy. Paul was inside it, inspecting its motor.

A dinghy? This is going to be a water-borne job?

Paul looked up as she approached.

'Hi Kerry.' He nodded. 'You all set?'

'Totally,' replied Venus, trying to figure out what on earth they were going to do.

'Mel's late.' Paul tutted.

The moonlight glinted on the water's surface illuminating the few solitary buildings at the river's side.

Five minutes later Mel appeared.

'You took your time,' Paul noted sarcastically.

'It's no big deal,' snapped Mel, muttering something under her breath.

'Right, get in you two,' Paul instructed them.

Mel went first and Venus followed.

'OK,' said Paul. 'We just need to wait for Franco.'

'Franco's coming tonight?' asked Venus. She felt physically sick.

'Yeah. Apparently his vendetta thing is nearly ready for action and the job tonight will help him.'

Venus felt a violent twist in her stomach. What on earth was she going to do?

Paul checked his watch. 'He'll be here in a minute.'

In spite of the coldness of the night, Venus could feel sweat breaking out all over her body.

At that second, she heard the low rumble of a vehicle's engine.

It's him!

The engine was getting louder and Venus spotted the front of a white van edging out from Fisherman's Way.

A terrible biting anxiety and fear of Franco ate away at her. She could be facing death at any minute. She needed to act fast – it might save her life.

'Here,' said Paul, reaching into a grey holdall, and

grabbing her attention for a second. He pulled out some black balaclavas and some pairs of thin black gloves. 'From now on we need to wear these.'

Venus had never been so happy to see a piece of headgear before. She slipped on the balaclava instantly. Then she pulled on the gloves; they were the sort that moulded to your hands whatever size they were.

I've got to stop freaking out. Calm down. Franco mustn't see how agitated I am.

A white van came into view and pulled up against a wooden fence. The engine was killed and five seconds later, Franco Dane appeared.

Venus felt a lump the size of a paving stone in her throat. After such a long build-up, she'd finally be at close quarters with him. It was completely hideous. Here, right here, was the person behind her worst nightmares. And he was after her. One false move and he'd know who she was. She gripped the side of the dinghy, trying not to feel overwhelmed.

Thank God for the balaclava!

Franco lumbered out of the van, slammed the door and pulled his own gloves and balaclava on, before stepping into the dinghy. He nodded to Paul and Mel and then turned to Venus.

'So you're the famous Kerry,' he said gruffly.

This was the first time Venus had come face-to-face

with Franco since he'd tried to kill her in the barn. She was completely terrified and had to work hard to control her nerves. If Franco realised it was her, Venus Spring, sitting by him, she had no doubt that he would kill her without hesitation.

Venus nodded.

'Paul is certainly impressed with you.'

Venus thought about disguising her voice in some way, but Paul and Mel had heard her speak plenty of times, so she just nodded again.

Franco's eyes stayed rooted on Venus; it felt like they were boring into her skull. *Has he recognised me from my eyes? Does he know it's me?*

The question burned in Venus's brain.

He held her gaze for a few more seconds and then spoke to them all.

'OK, listen carefully. The documents Paul photocopied relate to a shipping warehouse a couple of miles down the river,' he explained, moving his eyes between Paul, Mel and Venus.

'The bald guy with the briefcase is the warehouse manager. He always carries his documents round with him in that case. Paul copied inventories of stock – goods that have recently come in. Among those there are some incredibly expensive pieces of kit. And we're stealing them to order. All we need to do is get them out cleanly and quickly. I'll pass them over to our buyer who will pay top dollar to receive them.'

This is it; it's a robbery; this is my opportunity to get some evidence on Franco. But for God's sake, keep calm!

'Right,' declared Franco, pulling a sheet of paper out of his pocket. 'This is the layout of the warehouse.'

He turned the paper round so the others could see. It was a floor plan of the warehouse divided into numbered grids.

'The place has five warehouse units,' Franco explained. 'We're only going into Unit Four. Inside that warehouse there are twenty storage aisles with a central walkway cutting through them. That means there are forty different storage areas. We have some excellent information about the items' location – it's not a hundred per cent accurate, but it will get us to them pretty quickly.'

'Sounds like a bit of a nightmare,' muttered Mel.

Franco flashed her an angry stare – an expression that sent shivers shooting down Venus's spine. She obviously wasn't the only one who found Mel difficult.

'However,' Franco continued, 'from studying the inventories that Paul copied, we have reference numbers and descriptions of the goods we're targeting.'

'What about security?' asked Paul. 'Surely there'll be guards?'

'Of course there will be.' Franco nodded. 'There'll be two guards on tonight. One of them is our man on the inside, let's call him Guard X, and the other man is Guard Y. They alternate their breaks so there's always one of them in there. But that's going to change tonight.'

A wave lapped against the side of the dinghy and rocked it momentarily.

'At four-fifteen a.m., Guard Y will take a twenty-minute break. He'll leave his post and go to the little hut outside the warehouse where he and his colleagues make tea and things. The warehouse doors can only be opened by an authorised code that's changed every day, so Guard X can't just let us in through the front door – it will implicate him in the crime. We have another way in.'

'Hang on a sec,' ventured Paul. 'Isn't the time frame very short if we actually have to get in as well? Twenty minutes is nothing.'

Franco held up a finger. 'We'll have plenty of time,' he assured Paul. 'Trust me.'

Venus had to stop herself laughing out loud. *'Trust' and 'Franco' do not go together. He is the least trustworthy person I've ever met.*

'And our way in?' asked Paul.

'You'll see when we get there,' replied Franco.

'But won't Guard X still be implicated in the crime?' asked Mel. 'I mean, he'll be the one inside when we're there. Surely they'll know it's him.'

'Wrong,' said Franco. 'We'll rough the guy up a bit and tie him up. He'll look like a victim.'

This seemed to satisfy Mel.

Venus could feel the excitement and nerves bubbling inside her.

Franco checked his watch. 'Right, is everyone set?'

Venus, Paul and Mel nodded. Venus glanced down at her watch: 3.26 a.m. But she wasn't even vaguely tired – wired more like it.

'OK,' said Franco, 'let's do it.'

Paul pulled at a cord at the front of the dinghy and its motor scrambled to life. Venus watched as they pulled away from the shore. She turned to face the front and looked at the calm, moon-sparkling waters.

How the hell did I get myself involved in this – a well-planned night-time robbery? Is 'gathering evidence' enough to excuse me from the crime?

The dinghy was now cruising through the water. They passed several small boats tied up to landing stages and a couple of deserted, crumbling buildings. After ten minutes, they approached a series of five huge, slate-grey, inter-connected buildings on their right.

The shipping warehouses!

Franco cut the engine and let the dinghy glide silently to a long wooden jetty situated in front of a large square of tarmac that sat directly next to the grey buildings. There were wooden pallets strewn all over the yard that looked like large, discarded bits of Lego. It was obviously the loading yard for the warehouses.

Franco lifted his index finger and motioned for them to lean towards him. They all did so. Venus's face was now less than half a metre away from Franco's. She fought the urge to be sick.

'OK,' whispered Franco. 'I want each of you to go after one product.'

He handed each of them a piece of paper.

Venus looked at hers: *Nano DVD players: Aisle 19A or 20B. Dark blue boxes with silver crest at top right-hand corner; boxes marked Power Dash in corner. 10 players – no less.*

Mel looked at hers and then glanced over at Venus, who quickly folded hers and tucked it into her jacket pocket.

'What about you Franco?' asked Paul.

'Don't worry about me,' said Franco, a thin smile

curving on his lips. 'First I'll deal with the guard, then I'll go after my own haul. You guys just focus on your own jobs and we'll be fine.'

'What happens when Guard Y comes back?' asked Mel.

'He'll be back in by 4.35 a.m., yeah?' replied Franco. 'He'll find Guard X tied up, listen to the story he spins and call the police. We'll be long gone by then.'

'How do we move the stuff?' asked Paul. 'They're pretty big items.'

'Guard X says there are trolleys all over the place,' replied Franco. 'It'll all go smoothly. Anyone got any questions?'

No one said a word. Franco checked his watch again. 'We go in five minutes.' He then turned to face Venus. She could feel the sweat beneath her balaclava. 'And Kerry – no flash stuff. I've heard about your antics. You don't need to impress anyone. All you need to do is follow your instructions; got it?'

Venus nodded and tried to soothe her nerves.

The four of them got out of the boat and crouched down on the jetty. The five minutes seemed to take years. But finally Franco put a finger on his lips and nodded at the others.

With Franco at the front, they quickly started running down the jetty and across the loading yard. Venus jumped over the wooden pallets, watching her footing. The far side of the yard was a sloping concrete walkway. They followed it down. It snaked to the left with a metal walkway overhead. They scurried forward passing three large mesh panels on their left. Franco stopped at the fourth. They were now beneath Unit Four.

Venus looked at her watch: 4.09 a.m. *Six minutes and we're in.*

Franco pulled a screwdriver out of his jacket pocket and slipped its head underneath the bottom lip of the mesh panel. He slowly managed to lever it out. Several powerful tugs later and the first corner of the mesh had come free. After a minute the whole thing was off; Franco clearly knew exactly what he was doing.

Behind the mesh panel was a small steel door. Franco reached into his bag and pulled out a mini blow-torch. Paul, Venus and Mel edged back a bit. It was the work of thirty seconds to cut a big hole in the steel panel. Franco pushed his arm through and began unscrewing the screws on the inside that held the door. It came away in his hands. Behind the panel was darkness.

Venus checked her watch. 4.13 a.m.

'OK,' whispered Franco. 'Two minutes and we'll all be inside. No noise whatsoever.'

Franco then disappeared into the darkness. Mel went next. Then it was Venus's turn.

As she slipped forward into the pitch black, her hands immediately came into contact with the smooth steel surface of a shaft, which was obviously part of the ventilation system. It sloped upwards and was as easy to climb as a playground slide. As it was night-time, the system was off – making the shaft safe to traverse. As she moved upwards, the shaft became illuminated. Up ahead, she saw Franco and Mel on a steel platform where the slope levelled off. Franco had already taken off a mesh panel that led directly into the warehouse.

Venus glanced at her watch again: 4.15 a.m.

This is it!

She felt her heart hammering away inside her chest as if it was trying to break free from the shackles of her body. She could sense Paul behind her in the shaft. The seconds ticked by and then suddenly Franco was through. Mel shot after him as did Venus and Paul.

Venus got up quickly and took in the sight before her.

The warehouse was absolutely gigantic. It had stupendously high ceilings with arched wooden beams. Slivers of moonlight cut in through the high windows, looking like a series of torch beams. Stretching out in front of them was the central aisle with twenty sections – the A ones – on the left and twenty – the B ones – on the right, just as Franco had described it.

Venus took a quick look at the paper that she'd stowed in her jacket pocket.

Aisle 19A or 20B – dark blue boxes with silver crest. She then spotted a shadowy figure standing about forty metres away on her left.

'The guard,' Franco whispered. 'I'll deal with him; you guys go!'

Venus immediately began running down the central aisle with Mel and Paul. Wherever she looked there were towering piles of goods.

This stuff must be worth millions.

Paul stopped where the central path met Aisle 13A and scurried off.

Venus and Mel nodded and ran on. At Aisle 17A, Mel stopped and immediately began scouring the piles in that particular aisle. Venus continued until she got to Aisle 19A. She looked down it; it seemed to stretch forever.

OK, dark blue boxes with silver crests in your top right-hand corners; where are you?

Venus moved steadily down 19A, her eyes scanning every pile, searching for her targeted items. She took in each stack of goods carefully. She passed barbecue sets, games consoles, train sets and food processors. But no Nano DVD players. She reached the end of the aisle without luck. She checked her watch: 4.18 a.m. Then she turned and ran back to the central aisle and headed down 20B.

Here she hurried by remote control cars, dishwashers, hedge trimmers and fridge freezers, but still no DVD players. She felt the tension rising in her. *I have to find the damn things quickly.*

Finally at the end of 20B she spotted them – a towering stack of dark blue boxes bearing silver crests. She'd come back for them in a minute; first she wanted to see if she could find out what Franco was getting. As she moved on, she recalled Franco's words on the dinghy: *I'll deal with the guard; then I'll go after my own haul.*

Venus ran back to the central aisle and peered out. The coast was clear. She stepped out and crept back down the central aisle. Mel was halfway down Aisle 17A, reaching out to a large stack of boxes. Venus hurried past.

At 13B, she saw Paul. He had his back to her and was loading some steel cases on to a trolley.

Venus finally found Franco in Aisle 4A. For some reason, there was extra security on this aisle – Venus took in the extra gates and padlocks, the latter now cast on the ground next to some major wire cutters.

Franco was thirty metres down, crouching on the floor, a black, rectangular case about a metre long placed in front of him.

What's in the case?

Venus was absolutely determined to find out and she lost no time in heading down 5A. Between each pile of items was a narrow crack. If she could just get to the right section, she'd hopefully be able to take a closer look.

On she hurried, checking between all the gaps. She finally came exactly parallel to Franco. Between a tower of dishwashers and a mountain of mobiles on 5A was a thin crack, big enough for her to see Franco. He was kneeling on the ground now, inspecting the contents of the case. Venus cursed because the lid of the case obscured her view of what was inside. She checked her watch; 4.23 a.m. – time was moving too quickly.

She was just about to lean in further when she felt a rough hand on her shoulder. She spun round.

It was Mel. She was pushing a trolley loaded with purple boxes containing mini-laptops.

'What are you doing down there?' demanded Mel in a furious, accusing whisper.

'I was looking for this,' replied Venus, reaching out

to a trolley that was standing just behind Mel.

'But there were loads back there,' snapped Mel.

'I didn't see them,' lied Venus.

'What's happening?'

It was Franco's voice. Venus saw his eyes peering directly at her and Mel through the crack between 4A and 5A.

'It's nothing,' replied Venus, gruffly. 'We're just getting everything sorted.'

'Well get on with it!' urged Franco. 'We need to start loading the dinghy!'

Mel gave Venus another sour look and hurried away, pushing her trolley.

Venus checked her watch: 4.25 a.m. She hadn't collected her goods and she badly needed to get a move on. She grabbed the spare trolley, sped back to the central aisle and ran to Aisle 20B. With great urgency, Venus began loading the DVD players onto her trolley. But she could see pretty quickly that she wouldn't be able to get all ten on in one go. She cursed, loaded the eighth player and started racing to their entry point.

Franco's head was dipping out of the ventilation shaft. Mel was passing him goods and he was sliding them down the steel slope towards Paul at the bottom.

'We're nearly done,' Franco whispered when he saw Venus. 'Give us those ten and we'll be out of here.'

'There are only eight,' replied Venus.

Franco scowled. 'I told you to get ten.'

'Well you can only fit eight on one of these trolleys,' snapped Venus.

'Well go back and get the other two,' commanded Franco. 'We need all ten.'

Venus looked at her watch again: 4.29 a.m. Guard Y would be back in six minutes and would find Guard X tied up.

Venus shook her head, left the trolley next to Franco and sped back in the direction of Aisle 20B.

Instead of using a trolley, she grabbed two units off the pile and ran back to the central aisle with a DVD player tucked under each arm. She flew down the central aisle towards the open ventilation shaft. There was no sign now of Mel, Franco or Paul; Venus figured they must be at the bottom, busy loading the gear into the dinghy.

Venus had just run past Aisles 8A and 8B, when she heard the most ferocious splintering sound as the warehouse doors behind Aisles 20A and 20B were smashed in. Immediately there were shouts and yells and she saw a whole row of figures running towards her.

No, no, no, no no!

It was a whole line of security guards.

Venus felt as if her heart was about to explode.

What the hell is going on?

Venus ran, trying not to think about how many guards were tearing after her at this very moment? Five? Ten?

I have to get out of here! I HAVE to!

In desperation, she threw the two blue boxes onto the ground hoping that one or more of her pursuers would trip over them.

Who tipped them off, for God's sake? Franco said there'd only be two guards and one would stay on his break till 4.35 a.m! What's gone wrong?

With only a few metres to go to the ventilation shaft, Venus ran up some abandoned boxes and propelled herself forward into an airborne dive. Her body crashed into the ventilation shaft and she felt herself tumbling down the slope.

She emerged on the concrete walkway and ran hard until she reached the loading yard. In the distance she could see the three others, loading boxes into the dinghy. Past the scattered pallets she sprinted, flying past a fork-lift truck and kicking dust up with her trainers. The guards now emerged round the other side of the warehouse and pounded across the yard after her. There were only about forty metres to go. She took a quick look back. There were six of them, two of whom were closing in on her. She forced her burning muscles to give her more speed.

Venus now saw Franco chucking the last box into the dinghy and untying the ropes that held it to the jetty. Paul gestured to Franco, but Franco pushed him aside and grabbed the last rope. And then, to Venus's horror, she saw Mel pull at the engine cord and heard the noise of the dinghy's motor spluttering to life.

Oh my God! They're not going to wait for me!

She had twenty-five metres to go.

She could hear the rasping breath of the men on her tail. She leapt over two upturned pallets.

I'm pretty sure that Radcliff will bail me out if I get caught, but I've heard all sorts of stories about private security guards. They think they're above the law; they can be totally vicious. I've got to make it to the dinghy!

Venus was fifteen metres away from the dinghy now, but its motor was roaring angrily and it was pulling away from the side.

Come on! Come on!

Venus reached the jetty, the boards bowing under her feet. The dinghy was picking up speed fast.

But determination spurred Venus on. The dinghy was now some way away from the jetty, into the main wash of the water and Venus saw that in a few seconds any chance of her escaping would be gone.

As the end of the jetty neared and the footsteps of her pursuers thundered over the wooden planks behind her, Venus propelled herself through the air. It was just as well she was an excellent long jumper. She heard something plop into the water – had she dropped something? Too bad; she'd have to deal with that later. As her body arced through the air, she kicked out her legs and crashed onto the dinghy. Paul grabbed her by the elbow to steady her fall as the dinghy lurched first to the left and then to the right before steadying itself.

The cries and shouts from the panting guards on the jetty were soon left far behind.

'What the hell happened back there?' seethed Franco.

'You tell me!' shouted Venus quickly, her body shaking wildly.

'You could have blown the whole job!'

'It's not my fault!'

'You were the one who said we were clear till 4.35 a.m., Franco,' cut in Paul. 'I can't believe you were just going to leave Kerry there!'

'Sticking up for your girlfriend, are you?' barked Franco.

'Don't be stupid,' Paul thundered. 'If she hadn't been able to make that leap they'd have got her!'

'Shut up, Paul!' screamed Franco, the veins on his neck bulging like twisted worms.

'No, you shut up!' yelled Paul back, squaring up to Franco.

'STOP FIGHTING!'

It was Venus's turn to get a word in. All thoughts of Franco recognising her voice were temporarily pushed aside.

I've got to calm this situation right down, because getting Franco worked up like this is bound to end in trouble.

'None of that matters now,' she said lowering her tone. 'We got the stuff and we're out of there.'

'We didn't get *all* the stuff Kerry,' hissed Franco. 'I told you to get ten DVD players and you only got eight.'

'She would have got them if the alarm hadn't been raised,' snapped Paul.

'Look,' said Venus. 'They'll have a police helicopter and boats out in a few minutes. So why don't we just focus on getting back to the van, loading the stuff and splitting.' She'd spoken far more than she'd intended and although she'd tried to deepen her voice a little so that Franco wouldn't recognise it, she didn't want to arouse Mel and Paul's suspicions.

'Hear, hear,' said Paul with an encouraging nod at Venus.

Franco scowled at Venus and then at Paul. Slowly he turned to face Mel at the wheel.

The rest of the journey took place in silence. Venus couldn't stop shaking. This whole thing was turning into an absolute nightmare and if she could finish the night without ending up in a police cell or dead it would be a miracle.

All she could do was to stare at Franco's back and wonder what was in the slim black case that he'd been inspecting inside the warehouse – the same black case that was now resting at his feet.

Ten silent minutes later, Franco brought the dinghy into the landing stage. He and Mel got out quickly while Venus and Paul passed them the goods. As the four of them loaded the gear into the back of the van, they could hear the distant wail of police sirens.

'OK,' snapped Franco, 'no time for slushy goodbyes.'

He pulled off his balaclava. Paul and Mel copied him.

Venus felt her stomach hit the ground.

'We're off,' said Paul, turning to Venus. 'Are you coming with us in the van?'

If I take off my balaclava now, Franco will recognise me instantly!

'I'm fine on my own,' replied Venus quickly, backing away.

Franco narrowed his eyes, scrutinising Venus. 'Take off your balaclava,' he ordered, stepping towards her and reaching out his hand to pull it off.

Oh my God!

'Forget it! I'm not hanging round to get caught,' snapped Venus, pushing his hand away forcefully, before turning away and racing off in the direction of Fisherman's Way. As soon as she was out of sight, she stopped, and peered back around the wall.

'What are you playing at?' Franco called after her.

'Leave it, Franco!' shouted Paul.

At that moment, they heard another chorus of sirens.

'We're out of here!' cried Paul, leaping into the van with Mel. 'Are you coming Franco?'

'No!' snapped Franco. 'I've got stuff to do.'

As he walked away, Venus noticed that he hadn't put the black rectangular case in the van, along with everything else, but was carrying it. Whatever it held, its contents were of utmost importance to Franco – and Venus hadn't gone through the night's traumas to let him get away now.

Chapter Seven

Paul gunned the van's engine and floored the accelerator. Venus watched as the van careered off down the alleyway. A minute later, Franco stalked past where she was hidden.

Venus waited until he'd rounded the next bend in the alleyway and stole after him. Making sure her trainers only made the faintest sound on the cobbles, she followed from a distance of about thirty metres, hanging back in the shadows and never taking her eyes off his retreating back. He was clutching the black case tightly. What could possibly be in it? It had to be something valuable – jewellery perhaps?

Franco reached a small road, hurried down it and then came out onto a larger causeway. He dipped across this and disappeared into an underpass. Venus waited until he was almost at the other side before she entered. She then ran down it, just catching a glimpse of his retreating figure when she emerged. He took a left, two rights and then headed round the side of a tall mirror-fronted building.

At the main entrance to this building was a large glass wall with a black door set into it. Franco pulled out something that looked like a credit card and swiped it in a slot at the left side of the door.

The door swung open and he hurried inside. It shut quickly behind him. Venus watched as he crossed the marbled lobby and pressed the lift button. He waited for a minute, then the lift arrived and its door slid open. Luckily there was a digital panel above the door and Venus watched the numbers as the lift ascended. It stopped on the eleventh floor.

She looked at her watch. 5.05 a.m. Venus was completely exhausted, but she was determined to get into this building whatever it took.

Luckily it didn't take long.

Ten minutes later, as Venus stood freezing beside the building's entrance, a drunken couple in their twenties somehow managed to swipe their entrance card and open the door. They were so wrapped up in their own world that they didn't notice the teenage girl slip in behind them. They must have lived on the ground floor because they ignored the lift and turned left down the whitewashed corridor.

Venus pressed the lift call button, the doors opened and she stepped in and pressed 11. The doors shut smoothly and the lift began its ascent. On the eleventh floor, she stepped out and looked left and right; both ways led down whitewashed corridors.

What's the best way of finding where Franco went?

Venus turned to her left. There were ten flats this way. She walked down the corridor checking the names on the bells. There were seven couples' names. Venus couldn't be sure, but she felt pretty certain that Franco would be living alone – he was far too secretive to share his life with anybody. So that left three. One bell said Mabel Cleveland. The last two had male names: Eric Frost and Tony Chale.

He could be living under an alias. Venus took a look through both of these letterboxes. Eric Frost's flat had a suit hanging up on a peg in the hallway. Would Franco wear something like that? Unlikely, but possible. Tony Cheadle's hallway had hundreds of letters and leaflets scattered over the doormat and well beyond. Franco wouldn't leave all of that stuff there. So, on this side, Eric Frost seemed to be the only possible one.

Venus hurried down the other way. On this side there was also only one possible and this possible seemed far likelier than Eric Frost. This one's bell said Frank Dunne.

Frank/Franco? Surely no coincidence?

OK, what do I do now? Burst into Frank Dunne's flat screaming and shouting like in all of those cop films and catch Franco by surprise? Not in the state I'm in right now. No. I wait and watch him like a hawk.

Venus had been so preoccupied with checking out the flats and their occupants that she hadn't noticed the cupboard situated beside the lift. Now she tried its handle and it opened. There was a mop, a broom, several dustpans and brushes and lots of cleaning products. It must be a serviced building where everyone paid to have the corridors and walkways cleaned.

Venus found that by sitting inside the cupboard and partially closing the door, she could still see the corridor leading down to Frank Dunne's flat.

I need to check that it really is his flat. I need to see him come out of it.

Venus sat there leaning her back against a large wooden broom.

It's not exactly five-star comfort, but it will have to do.

As she sat there she went over the events of the last few hours: the meeting at the landing stage, the coming face-to-face with Franco, the ventilation shaft, the warehouse, the running away from the guards, and finally the black case resting at Franco's feet.

It wasn't long before she felt her eyelids drooping.

Absolutely no way am I going to fall asleep.

A couple of times, she gave herself a short slap in the face to fend off sleep, but she simply couldn't stop her eyelids shutting.

Venus awoke, her neck aching, her bones leaden and her mouth feeling like it was stuffed with wool. She checked her watch. 9.05 a.m. She cursed aloud.

How could I have fallen asleep?

She hurried down the corridor to Frank Dunne's flat where she pressed her ear against the ricketty door and listened. There was no sound from inside, but that could mean anything. He was probably still asleep.

'He's not in.'

Venus spun round. A woman in a black and white checked skirt suit was in the hall, obviously on her way out.

'The guy in number 117 – that is who you're looking for, isn't it?'

Venus nodded. 'Yeah,' she said, 'tall guy, brown hair.'

The woman nodded. 'I saw him leave about ten minutes ago. I was just going out but then the phone rang.'

'Right.' Venus smiled weakly. 'Er, thanks for that.'

Venus waited until the woman had gone, and then turned back and hurried to the door to Franco's flat. She tried it, and though it was locked, it didn't feel completely secure. She stood back a few paces and smashed her shoulder into the door exactly at the weakest lock point, just as Dennis had showed her on set countless times, with a terrific thud. It creaked a bit, but that was all. She looked round to see if the noise had alerted anyone, but there was no one around. She stood further back and repeated the exercise; the door smashed open and Venus fell inside.

Venus found herself in a small hallway with doors opening off from it. The first room she went into was the sitting room.

She felt a chill steal over her heart and her breath catch in her throat. There, covering the entire left wall of the room, were photos, maps and notes. There were plenty of photos of her – walking out of her front door, standing with Kate Fox outside the school gates, cycling down the road. But what was even more disturbing was the fact that photos of her only accounted for about a quarter of the wall's surface. The other three-quarters were covered in photos of . . . her mum.

There were literally hundreds of them: some were grainy black and white shots, others were sepia-tainted and the rest were crisp digital snaps. They covered every aspect of Gail's life, from her arriving at the gym to her putting empty milk bottles on the front doorstep last thing at night.

Venus stared at this display of the Spring family with her mouth wide open and a terrible sick feeling in the pit of her stomach. She moved closer, feeling her legs shaking. The maps and notes were all connected to Venus and particularly Gail's movements and timetables. There were maps of Gail's route to work, a detailed diagram of her office and information on every destination Gail had recently visited.

Venus tried hard to piece together what was happening. Why were there pictures of Gail on the wall? Why her mother? Franco hated her, not her mum, didn't he?

And then Venus saw the black rectangular case Franco had taken from the warehouse, lying open on the floor.

She hurried over, knelt down beside it and lifted the lid. It was empty. But it contained several sections where different items could be stored: a long thin one, a small square one, a circular piece with a kind of stem. Venus gasped as she recognised what would be stored there – she'd seen several fake ones on film sets. It was a gun. It was a sniper rifle – or rather an empty case for one. Franco must have the gun with him!

And then suddenly a dreadful realisation hit her. Franco wasn't after *her*. No. He believed Venus had killed his mother and in retaliation he was going to kill . . . Venus felt faint and slumped against the wall. Franco had been watching her, but it was *Gail* he was after – he wanted to make Venus suffer in the same way as him.

As these terrifying thoughts hurtled through Venus's brain, she fumbled anxiously in her jacket for her mobile. Her fingers felt round inside the pockets but no phone appeared. She tried the pockets of her jeans, but still no phone. A sickening realisation hit her in the chest. *My phone must have fallen out of my jacket when I jumped off the jetty into the dinghy.*

Venus looked desperately round the flat, but there was no phone. She raced out of the door and down the corridor. She couldn't wait for the lift to come so she leapt down the stairwell, taking four steps at a time. As soon as she hit the ground floor she rushed to the front door and hit the access switch on the left that opened the door from the inside.

She burst into the street, the panic rising by the second.

What if I'm too late? I'll never, ever, forgive myself.

She looked in both directions for a phone box but there was none.

I HAVE to find a phone immediately!

Venus ran and finally came across a silver phone box. Relieved, she picked up the receiver. The phone was dead. Aaargh!

A woman walked by at that second, talking into her mobile.

Venus raced after her and tapped on her shoulder. 'I'm really, really sorry, but I NEED to use a phone,' panted Venus. 'It's an emergency!'

The woman turned round and gave Venus a harsh stare.

'PLEASE!' pleaded Venus. 'I'm DESPERATE.'

The woman sighed deeply and spoke into the receiver. 'Listen, Cathy, someone needs to borrow my mobile urgently, I'll call you back in a minute.'

'Thank you,' blurted out Venus, grabbing the phone. In an instant she'd dialled Gail's mobile. It was answered after three rings.

'Hello?'

'Mum, it's me.'

'Hi, hon, how are you doing? How was the party?'

'Where are you, Mum?'

The reception wasn't great. There was a humming noise and faint crackling.

'Is everything OK?' asked Gail. 'Is it the bad line or do you sound stressed?'

'WHERE ARE YOU?' Venus shouted.

'Why, hon?'

'Please, Mum, just tell me where you are!'

The crackle on the line got louder and was now accompanied by an infuriating buzzing sound.

'I'm on my way to see a client.'

'But it's Sunday!'

'You know I sometimes have Sunday appointments. It's been in my diary for ages.'

Venus could just about hear Gail's answer but the line was breaking up badly.

'Where?' demanded Venus breathlessly. 'Where is the appointment?'

'This line's terrible Venus. I'm going to . . .'

Gail said something that Venus couldn't hear.

'WHERE?' shouted Venus.

'Fenford Prison,' replied Gail. It sounded vaguely familiar.

'Listen, Mum,' said Venus trying desperately to sound calm, 'You mustn't go th—'

'Sorry,' interrupted Gail, 'you're breaking up. What did you say?'

'MUM!' yelled Venus, 'YOU MUSTN'T GO THERE!'

'I can't hear you, hon. I'll see you at home, later.'

'I SAID YOU MUSTN'T GO TO FENFORD PRISON. TURN BACK NOW!'

But the line had gone completely dead. She dialled her mum's number again, but there was just a voice saying the number was unavailable.

I can't believe this is happening! What am I going to do?

The woman looked concerned. 'Are you all right?'

Venus's hands were trembling furiously now as she dialled Radcliff's number. She'd learnt it off by heart for emergencies.

'DCI Radcliff's office,' answered a businesslike, female voice after two rings.

'Can I speak to DCI Radcliff please?'

'She's not here at the moment, can I get her to call you back?' said the voice.

Venus tried to modulate her own voice so that she didn't sound like a screaming banshee.

'It's an emergency,' she said.

'Then I suggest you dial 999,' replied the woman.

Venus felt like pounding the phone against a wall.

'It's not that kind of emergency!' she insisted.

'Look,' said the voice firmly, 'it either is an emergency or it's not. If it is, call 999, if it's not then you'll just have to leave a message for the DCI.'

'OK,' said Venus, 'can you put me through to her voice mail?'

There's no way I'm going to trust this officious woman with a message.

'Yes I can – putting you through now.'

A few seconds later she heard Radcliff's voice mail message. Venus quickly left a message and flung the mobile back to its owner, with a quick 'Thanks'.

'Are you sure you're OK?' asked the woman. But Venus had no time for the courtesy of an answer. The clock was ticking and this was a matter of life and death.

As Venus pounded down the street, she racked her brains to try and dredge up any information her brain had stored on Fenford Prison. By the time she'd reached the nearest tube station, she'd remembered where she'd seen the name before – she'd read it in Gail's work diary the night she had heard the thudding noise in her office and went to investigate. Franco must have been in there. He knew Gail's schedule. He must be going to trail her there. But she had no idea where the prison was.

'Do you know where Fenford Prison is?' she blurted out to the guard who was standing by the automatic passenger barriers.

He pulled a face. 'No idea,' he replied, turning to a colleague who was standing a few metres away. 'Where's Fenton Prison?'

'FENFORD!' said Venus, forcing herself not to lose her temper.

'Go to Argyle Broadway,' said the other guard.

'Thank you!' cried Venus, swiping her train pass and running through the metallic barriers. She sped down the moving escalator.

'Hey!' shouted a man carrying a young child, after Venus's elbow had caught him on the back. She didn't even turn round to apologise. All she could think of was Franco, her mother and Fenford Prison.

She burst onto the platform. *NEXT TRAIN 4 MINUTES* declared the orange letters on the digital display board.

Hurry up! Hurry up!

The four minutes dragged by with agonising slowness. Venus's whole body was wired. She tapped her feet on the floor, and clenched and unclenched her fists repeatedly. Finally the *TRAIN APPROACHING* sign appeared. The train emerged nosily from the tunnel and stopped.

Venus got into a carriage that was empty save for a man with a guide dog. She stayed standing; she was too worked up to sit down. It was eleven stops to Argyle Broadway. She looked at her watch. 10.01 a.m. What time was Gail's meeting? Would Venus get there in time or would she end up visiting a murder scene?

The train made several long stops in stations, which

simply added to Venus's spiralling anxiety. Passengers got on and off but Venus took no notice of them. She was just trying to keep calm.

Finally, forty-five minutes later, the train pulled into Argyle Broadway. Venus leapt out of the carriage and was the first passenger up the stairs. Pelting through the ticket barriers she saw a sign tacked to the wall. *FENFORD PRISON ONE MILE*, it informed her, with an arrow pointing to the left.

Venus found herself on a cobbled walkway that ended in a quiet residential road. Beyond this was a long stretch of open grass with a path cutting through the middle. This was the way to Fenford Prison. It had been built just outside town. Venus had a mile to cover and knew she needed to do it with Olympian speed. Her feet pounded over the path, beads of sweat trickling down her forehead, determination etched on her face.

Straight ahead of her was an imposing grey building, with very high walls and razor wire stretching above them.

That must be it. That's Fenford Prison.

Spurred on by this realisation Venus sprinted even faster. She covered the ground incredibly quickly. Sure enough, the building standing directly in front of her bore a sign saying: *H.M.PRISONS – FENFORD*.

Running off to the left along the front of the prison

was a track. There was no sign of anyone on this. To the right was another track; again this was clear.

OK, think, THINK!

Venus gazed up at three buildings on the right. The one furthest away from the prison was derelict. The second was occupied; Venus could see workers inside sitting at computer terminals. That left the building nearest to the prison.

This one also looked empty, but a sign draped across its front stated: *MAJOR REDEVELOPMENT PROJECT: OFFICE SPACE FOR HIRE; CALL JOHN COULSEN*. It listed three phone numbers.

She took a step back and spun round to get a three hundred and sixty degree panoramic view.

Where the hell is he? And where the hell is Mum?

Venus's whole body was taut with terror. How many minutes did she have? It might only be seconds. Images of all the photos on Franco's wall ripped through her mind. Did she still have a chance to save her mum's life?

Venus desperately looked up at the redeveloping office block.

Give me a sign – anything! COME ON!

And that's when she saw something glinting out of a high window. It took her a few seconds to realise what it was and, when she did, her heart gave a lurch.

It was the end of a gun barrel. It would have been easy to miss as it only protruded a few centimetres, but she could see it clearly – she was used to sizing up the smallest details on a stunt.

Venus's heart thumped even faster.

She stole a look at the left and right pathways in front of the prison; there was still no sign of anyone.

Where are you, Mum?

Venus ran to the front glass doors of the office block that was being refurbished. One of them was open. She hurried through and crashed up the stairwell. It was a very tall building; there were approximately fifteen floors and Venus had zero time to waste. Huge windows were on her left. She sped up four floors, then five, then six. On each floor she took a quick look down the corridor. Every single door in these corridors was shut.

Her heart was hammering in her chest and blood was pounding her ears whilst her whole body was pulsing with adrenaline as she waited to hear the sound of a gun being fired: a bullet that would end her mum's life.

When I was outside why didn't I count the number of floors and work out which one he's on? How could I have been so damn stupid?

Venus scrambled past the seventh floor, then the

eighth. She was just about to reach the ninth floor when she spotted something out of one of the massive windows to her left: her mum.

Venus felt a sharp pain in her chest.

Gail was striding confidently forward. Venus stopped running immediately and with both fists pounded on the windows.

'MUM!' she yelled.

But Venus could see that Gail was wearing her tiny iPod headphones and was totally engrossed in a song. It would take a bomb blast to summon her attention when those headphones were on. Venus smashed her fists against the window again, but Gail didn't even look up. Again and again Venus hit the toughened glass, but still she couldn't get her mum's attention.

This could be the last time I ever see her alive. Please Mum. Look up for just a second.

Tears streamed down Venus's cheeks as she hammered the window one last time. Gritting her teeth with fury and determination, Venus raced up the next two flights of stairs, past floor nine and floor ten. At floor eleven she skidded to a halt. One of the doors was slightly open, allowing a thin beam of light out into the corridor.

Venus's fists were clenched tight and every sinew of her body was ready to face Franco. At this second, Gail

Spring would be reaching the front entrance of Fenford Prison and Franco would be taking a shot at her to exact his revenge.

Venus ran to the open door and looked inside. There, on the far side of the room was Franco. He was kneeling down with a sniper's rifle pointing out of the window. The whole scene suddenly seemed to take on a blurry, slow-motion quality for Venus. She sprinted across the room, watching Franco curl his finger round the gun's trigger, about to squeeze it. A few metres away Venus threw herself into the air just as his trigger finger began to squeeze down. A nanosecond before he completely depressed his finger, Venus landed a full impact kick on his back.

Suddenly everything sped up again.

Franco pulled the rifle's trigger. The bullet tore through the window sending shards of glass outwards.

'NOOOO!' screamed Venus.

Franco and Venus crashed to the ground. Instantly Franco wriggled to the side and elbowed Venus in the midriff. But she had tensed her stomach muscles in preparation and the blow didn't destabilise her. Franco leapt back onto his feet, lifted the gun and prepared to take another shot at Gail. But Venus was already on her feet and she threw a punch at his trigger hand. The gun swung violently to the left, releasing a second bullet and destroying another huge pane of glass. Venus looked out of the window. Gail was lying prostrate on the pavement outside the front of the prison.

NO! PLEASE NO! HE'S KILLED HER!

At that second, Franco hit her in the face with the butt of his gun. Venus screamed and staggered backwards from the searing pain.

His fingers curled tightly round the gun, as if it were a club.

Venus's cheek felt like it had been burnt.

'YOU KILLED MY MUM!' she shouted, her heart pounding with agony, her voice croaky.

'Fair's fair!' he shouted, with a mad gleam in his eyes. 'You killed MY mum!'

'I didn't kill her!' screamed Venus through her tears. 'It was an accident!'

'It was your fault. So finally justice has been done!'

Venus made a sudden move to punch him, but he blocked her and shoved her backwards. She kept her balance and leapt back at him, catching him full in the face with a mighty kick. He yelled in agony and almost dropped his gun, but he kept his grasp and brought it back towards Venus's head for another blow. She ducked and he swung at thin air. Before he could get his bearings again, she spun round and let fly with a roundhouse kick to his ribs. He flew backwards, knocking over a stepladder and some empty tins of paint.

But before Venus could reach him again, he raised the gun barrel and aimed it directly at her head.

Venus froze.

His finger hovered over the trigger.

Now he's going to kill me! Well if Mum is dead, maybe that's the best thing.

But from somewhere very deep inside, Venus found herself summoning her last ounce of strength. She twisted her body to the right as a bullet split the air beside her. It smashed through a wall. She pulled to the side but instead of running away, she ran straight towards Franco. He lifted the gun as he re-aimed at her heart, and in the second he looked down Venus propelled herself up and caught Franco straight on with a full-force flying kick to his face. Franco howled in fury and dropped the gun as he clutched his face. Venus saw her chance and dropped to a crouch, clearing the gun out of reach with one sweeping kick. Before Franco realised what was happening, she had him face down on the floor with both of his arms pinned behind his back.

'LET GO OF ME!' he screamed. 'LET GO!'

'YOU KILLED MY MUM!' Venus screamed. 'YOU KILLED MY MUM!'

She was crying and screaming and shaking. But her grip held and he stayed pinned to the floor – his gun well out of reach.

The image of Gail spread out on the ground outside flooded her mind and she sobbed uncontrollably.

But a second later, the sound of deep voices yelling, 'POLICE – ARMED RESPONSE!' filled the room. Six police officers wearing body armour and hard hats fanned out in a semi-circle, their semi-automatic machine guns trained on Franco.

'STAY DOWN!' yelled one of the officers, at the same time as indicating with for Venus to stand up. She did so very slowly, with her hands raised.

And then another figure walked into the room.

DCI Radcliff.

She nodded at one of the officers. Immediately two of them walked over to Franco and dragged him to his feet. In a second, one of them snapped a pair of handcuffs round his wrists. He stood there, with grime smeared across his forehead, fury and despair etched on his face.

'It's not over,' he hissed at Venus.

'Save your words for the judge,' commanded Radcliff in a cold, clear tone.

Franco stared at her in disgust.

'Take him away,' instructed Radcliff.

The six officers, with Franco in their midst, left the room.

It was suddenly very quiet.

'Are you OK?' asked Radcliff, stepping over to Venus.

'My mum,' sobbed Venus, 'she's d . . . d . . . dead.'

'No I'm not.'

Venus spun round. There in the doorway was Gail Spring.

Venus felt like she was going to explode with emotion. She rushed towards her mother and was swept up in a gigantic hug. Her body was shaking violently but her tears of agony had turned to tears of incredible relief.

After about a minute, Gail tried to pull away, but Venus wouldn't let her go. It was only thirty seconds later that they finally parted.

'I thought you were dead,' said Venus hoarsely.

'I hit the ground, the second I heard the bullet,' said Gail. 'After the second shot, I ran across to the doorway of this building. I saw the police storming into the building and I heard one of them mention your name. I thought *you'd* been shot. I ran up after them.'

DCI Radcliff gave Venus an encouraging smile. 'There are some things I need to do, Venus,' said the policewoman. 'I'll see both you of downstairs, OK?'

Venus nodded but Gail frowned deeply. She waited until Radcliff had left the room.

'That police woman sounded like . . . like she knows you,' said Gail with a look of bewilderment. 'Or am I just imagining it? And my God, Venus, what happened to your face?'

A cut was bleeding on Venus's cheek.

Venus felt her legs buckling beneath her and she slid down onto the floor, resting her back against the wall. Gail joined her and they sat side by side amongst the dirt and dust.

'Venus,' said Gail. 'How on earth did you get mixed up in this whole thing? Are you going to tell me what the hell is going on? '

Venus took a very deep breath and composed herself before she replied.

'I think so. . .'

'Yes?' Gail said expectantly.

'Mum,' Venus began, 'I think there are quite a few things I need to tell you . . .'

Experience Venus's other adventures!

Stunt Girl
JONNY ZUCKER

Venus leapt from the platform like a springing cheetah, pumping her legs in mid-air as she'd seen long-jumpers do. There were gasps from the people below – there was no way she could make it across without a rope. She hung in the air as if suspended, as if for a second she'd bypassed the laws of time and gravity.

Venus Spring is fourteen and this is the first summer she'd been allowed to go to stunt camp. It is a dream come true, something she has been working towards for years. But while she is there, she stumbles on a devious and terrifying plot that threatens the surrounding countryside, and Venus is determined to uncover it.

'An exciting page-turner that will have you gripped!' MIZZ

'A fast-paced, thrilling read.' The Sunday Times

ISBN: 978 1 85340 837 3

Body ★ Double

JONNY ZUCKER

The man turned round to face Venus with a start, but he was too late. Venus's feet thudded against the top section of the perimeter wall, allowing her to grab the man's jacket and pull it as hard as she could. He let out a startled cry as they tumbled down together and crashed on to the hedge.

When DCI Radcliff hears a rumour that a gang intends to kidnap teen movie star Tatiana Fairfleet, she asks Venus to act as Tatiana's body double at her boarding school – providing a decoy if there are any problems. But Venus soon finds herself in real danger, and will need to rely on all her stunt skills if she is to stop events spiralling out of control.

'Exciting and fast paced, you'll be wowed by her daring antics.'
MIZZ

ISBN: 978 1 85340 873 1

Star ✷ Turn

JONNY ZUCKER

Venus gritted her teeth and sped forward at full throttle. She was gaining on the red motorbike, going as fast as she could. Whatever she did, she mustn't lose them. Whoever was on that bike could be vital to the investigation.

When Venus Spring's estranged father turns up unexpectedly, her world is thrown into turmoil. As she gets to know him, she finds herself drawn into his investigative work, involving a major player in the film industry.

But Venus's opportunity to finally be a stunt girl turns into a nightmare as she discovers a deadly secret . . .

'Fab, cool and funny.' MIZZ

ISBN: 978 1 85340 902 8

Discover more Piccadilly Pearl books

SAXBY SMART
PRIVATE DETECTIVE

THE CURSE OF THE ANCIENT MASK
and other case files

SIMON CHESHIRE

My name is Saxby Smart and I'm a private detective. I go to St Egbert's School, my office is in the garden shed, and these are my case files.

In this book Saxby solves three of his most puzzling cases: The Curse of the Ancient Mask, The Mark of the Purple Homework and The Clasp of Doom. In each story Saxby gives you, the reader, clues which help solve the mystery. Are you 'smart' enough to find the answers?

'Talk about being involved in a book! Sharp reads written in a lively and snappy style.' Liverpool Echo

ISBN: 978 1 85340 943 1

Sea Girls
The Crystal City

g.g. elliot

As Polly dived into the pool, the water went straight up her nose. Normally this would make her choke and gasp for air, but this time some instinct made her suck the water through her nose and push it out of her mouth. She could breathe underwater!

Even before this, Polly had always felt different. But then she finds a kindred spirit in Lisa, who she meets at a swimming competition. The two girls discover that they both have the same fish-shaped birthmark, were both adopted, and can both breathe underwater. Surely it can't just be coincidence?

When a strong current drags them to the depths of the ocean, they not only discover their true identities, but an amazing world – more incredible and more disturbing than they could ever have imagined . . .

'It's got mystery, a magical new world and it's got excitement oozing from its gills.' Liverpool Echo

ISBN: 978 1 85340 878 6

www.piccadillypress.co.uk

☆ The latest news on forthcoming books

☆ Chapter previews

☆ Author biographies

☆ Fun quizzes

☆ Reader reviews

☆ Competitions and fab prizes

☆ Book features and cool downloads

☆ And much, much more . . .

Log on and check it out!

Piccadilly Press